Hush the Cries of a White Dove

by

Aly DeRay

Table of Contents

Acknowledgments

First of all, I would like to thank Ondi Laure and Persona Publishing Company, for making my lifelong dream come true.

I am very thankful for my children, who have always been patient with me when I was writing and let me finish a paragraph before they would interrupt me. They have always believed it me and for that, I am eternally grateful.

I want to thank my two, very best, lifelong friends, Tammy and Denise, for helping me to find the courage I needed to put my writings out to the world.

To my mother and late father, I thank you from the bottom of my heart, for the faith you have always had in me and the never ending support you have given me, throughout every stage of my life.

I love you all!

Chapter 1

Northwestern Nebraska Territory
mid-1800s…

A chorus of crickets fell to a brief silence as the hoof beats of a horse with his rider drew near. The steady thumps also brought the attention of a colony of prairie dogs who came up out of their dens and stood tall on hind legs to see what was causing such a disturbance. A sage hen flew up in the distance, followed by the cry of a hawk as it soared above them. Accompanying the rhythmic beats came the steady pants of the horse's breath, each creating its own puff of steam that rose up and quickly dissipated into the crisp, cool morning air. The dew-soaked grass glistened in the sun's early light, resembling thousands of tiny diamonds spread all across the land. A gentle, light fog blanketed the nearby pond, and in the silence of the morning, the rider could hear the calm chatter of the ducks concealed beneath.

At the moment the horse came to a stop, the ducks grew silent. It was a very brief silence, though, for almost as suddenly as it quieted, the commotion of excitement commenced.

They had become aware of the intruder's presence. The noise began with erratic splashes of water followed by wild and clamorous honking that sent echoes throughout the valley. The ducks appeared in groups, out from under the blanket and onto the bank of the pond as the rider dismounted. "Fury," she giggled as she stroked her horse's neck, "I think we've been discovered." The unconcerned equine bent his head down and grabbed a mouthful of the drenched, succulent vegetation that taunted him all the way here.

She removed her gloves and placed them on the saddle, then reached into her pocket for the small bag of breadcrumbs and corn kernels to feed to the apparently starved fowl. They were bold and greedy as they pushed and grabbed, fearlessly pecking around her boots to gobble up any morsels of the crumbs she allowed to fall. Kathleen giggled joyfully at their antics as she tossed a little here and a little there, in an attempt to give the slower and smaller ones a chance to get bits of the treat. No matter how full her bag was, it never seemed to be enough. It was impossible to know if any had gone without, but as soon as the ducks realized the donations were gone, they slowly lumbered back to the water's edge. Quietly, they chatted to one another as they settled back into the water to resume their peaceful morning swim. They appeared careless and casual as they seemed to pick up where their previous conversations had left off, as though they had never even been interrupted in the first place.

For as long as she had been old enough to ride, Kathleen had come out to this pond nearly every morning to visit and feed the many generations of ducks that nested here during the warmer months of the year. The tradition began with her mother.

Just over twenty-five years ago, when her parents married, they came to live on the ranch, and when her mother, Anna, became familiar with the land, she began to ride daily. When Kathleen was about two years old, her mother began to bring her along, and it became their tradition. Just after the rooster's first crow and as the sun's rays showed the first glint of light, the family rose from their beds to start the activities of the busy day that lay ahead. After a hearty breakfast, the men of the family went to the barns and stables to begin their work, and the women went for their ride. This was a time for mother and daughter to be alone, to talk of things that only they could share. At the house, there were the men and the hired workers. This was their time and theirs alone, and they used it avidly, to create special memories they could cherish forever.

Now, this time was just for Kathleen, to remember her mother and to hold dear the bond they shared. It was a peaceful time to sit and listen to the day's beginning stirs of nature. It was the time of day to take a deep breath and feel the cool, moist air enter and refresh her body, to feel the gentle breeze in her hair and the sun's first warm rays on her face. It was the peaceful time of day…normally.

Suddenly, Fury's head came up with a jerk, his ears perked forward, and he let out a low nicker. He heard something. He stopped chewing on the buffalo grass that filled his mouth and stood very still to listen. Kathleen stood and turned in the direction the horse stared, and she also became motionless. Suddenly, she heard it too. The sound of hoof beats grew louder as they rapidly drew near. Within seconds, they saw them as they rose over the hill and raced toward them in full speed lope.

Fury let out a panic-stricken whinny as Kathleen ran up the bank to where he stood by the large oak tree. Impatiently, he pranced as she mounted, then they turned in the direction of the house, and Fury ran as fast as he could go. Kathleen leaned into him, as she had been taught by her father, to give him less restriction and full range of motion, which enabled him to run faster. She could hear the other horse behind her now. He was closing in. "Come on boy," she pleaded. "Faster! They're gaining!" Fury let out a snort, and Kathleen could feel his muscles bulge and his body stretch as he tried to pick up speed. The ground was familiar to him as he galloped along. He had this route memorized and knew every rock, bush, and crevice along the way. This was to their advantage, for when Kathleen glanced behind them, she could see the other horse fall behind. But not too far, and not for long. She could hear the rider as he gave commands, and soon the black stallion began to close the distance between them again. Kathleen began to panic. "Fury, they're going to catch us. Go faster! Please, go faster!" she begged him. Just as she turned to see how close they were to them, Kathleen's father's horse flew past Fury as if he trotted at a steady gait.

"Ah ha!" Martin called back over his shoulder, and he threw his hands up victoriously. "I told you old Prince still had it in him!" He laughed, then hollered and cheered as they sped on to the barnyard, which was just ahead in the near distance.

Kathleen and Fury relaxed now, and they slowed to a peaceful, casual walk. She leaned forward again, stroking his wet, sweating neck, and reassured him. "That's alright, Fury. We don't like to run anyway, do we?" The horse shook his head and let out a loud sighing snort, as if to respond to her question. Kathleen smiled and rose up in her saddle to wave at her father, who gloated about his win. "Yeah, yeah, we know," she replied, but only loud enough for Fury to hear. She could hear her father call to her, and as he did, he waved both hands in the air. It no longer seemed like a victory dance when he was joined by Max, who began to shout and wave along with him. Kathleen knew something had happened. They were still about a half-mile away, so she coaxed Fury into a trot to get there a little faster, to appease them and to satisfy her own rising curiosity as to what the excitement was about.

When she arrived, she was greeted by Tommy, a stable boy, who took Fury and led him to the stalls to be groomed and fed. Her father and Max smiled as they gave her the news of most recent birth on the ranch. Monarch, Kathleen's own Arabian mare, had finally given birth to a healthy new colt. She was relieved the news was good and that the baby was healthy and strong. This was her mare's first foal, and when the birth went well over two weeks past due, everyone began to get a little anxious. "All is well," Martin assured her, "and to be on the safe side, we'll have Doc Carter come out and give them both a full physical examination." He put his arm around her and squeezed her tight as he laughed aloud happily.

"Thank you, Daddy," she replied as she hugged him back. Then she walked to Max and gave him a big hug as well. "And thank you, too, Max." She gave the man a little kiss on his sweaty, dusty cheek. "I'll bet you were up half the night with her, weren't you?"

"No." Max raised his shoulders and shrugged as though it was no big deal, then added, "I was up *all* night with her!" Playfully, he rolled his eyes back, sank to the ground, and lay in the dirt, as if he had passed out from sheer exhaustion. They all laughed as Max got back up and brushed the dust from his trousers. "You don't have to thank me, my lady." He removed his hat and bowed. "It is what I do." He smiled up at her.

She smiled, and as she pretended to lift her imaginary skirts, she curtsied and giggled at his gesture. "Now then," she cleared her throat, "what's a lady have to do to get one, or both"—she eyed them back and forth—"of you fine gentlemen to escort her into the stables to see this new little prince?" She playfully batted her long, full eyelashes.

Max laughed then swatted Martin on the arm with his hat. "You two go on ahead," he respectfully declined. "I'd love to accompany you both, but I need to get cleaned up and get some food in my belly. Work's awaitin'." As he turned to walk away, he added, "I'm afraid, for some odd reason, I've fallen way behind on my chores this morning."

"Go take a nap, Max!" Martin ordered him, but he knew his words would not be heard. Max was a fine man, a hard worker, and much too devoted to his job to ever take time off. He knew there were plenty of men there to do the work that needed to be done, but Max was the foreman. He loved his job and the responsibilities that came with it. He also knew problems could arise and exciting things could happen at any moment, and he couldn't stand the thought of missing a minute of any of it. Besides, the excitement of a new birth always got his blood pumping and his adrenaline going. He'd never be able to sleep now, even if he tried.

As Max trudged toward the small grove of trees where his cabin was, Martin asked Tommy to go and fetch him some food. "Yes, sir," Tommy replied with a smile, then ran down the road toward the main house. Her father turned to Kathleen and held out his elbow for her to take. He smiled and asked her, "Shall we?"

Happily, she took his arm. "Let's," she giggled in reply, and then allowed him to escort her in the direction of the birthing stable.

Once inside, they found the foal as he tried to stand for his first time. Monarch continued to lick him clean, and as she did so, she tried to help steady his wobbly legs. Kathleen couldn't help but be astonished at how much the foal resembled his sire, Prince of the Sahara, Martin's Arabian stallion. Monarch was a bay, and Prince was a shiny, satiny coal black, except for a crown-shaped white spot on his forehead and a large white spot that covered the total lower half of his left hind foot. The foal was the same glossy black, and his left hind foot had the same white spot, but the mark on his forehead was more of a lightning bolt. It started at his forehead and zigzagged to almost a point at the tip of his nose.

Kathleen was lost in his beauty and in thoughts of a magnificent name, when her father nudged her. "Looks like old Prince has created himself some competition, huh?" he whispered. She nodded in agreement, then a thought came to mind and she smiled at the vision of victory over her father in a race for home, riding on the adult-sized Blaze of Glory.

Later that morning, after Kathleen had cleaned up and changed her clothes, Martin asked her to accompany him into town. He wanted to talk to the veterinarian about the new foal's physical examination, as well as the needed attention of some other ailing animals on the ranch. Kathleen happily accepted his invitation, as she loved to go into town and mingle with the people. Her brother owned and operated the town's mercantile, and there was Billie Jean, who worked at the post office. Clara and Sue were waitresses at one of the hotel's restaurants in Augusta, and her dearest friend Lana would be at home, tending to her ailing grandmother. Her father's visits with the good doctor were never brief, as they had been friends for over 30 years, ever since they had attended the country school together. Now they would get out the cigars and brew some coffee and talk for hours on the doctor's office steps. Kathleen had nearly the rest of the day to visit with all of her friends.

Once in town, they found it was a busy place for everyone. Small groups of people chatted on the sidewalks, small children raced around at play, while pedestrians, horse- pulled buggies, and wagons crowded the streets. Martin carefully made his way to the mercantile first to drop Kathleen off at the steps in front of the building. Here was where they found Joshua, leaned back in his chair with his feet propped up on the porch's banister, as he read the daily newspaper.

"Busy day?" Martin jested with a chuckle.

"Hey, Pop!" Joshua sat up in a hurry and dropped his paper to the porch. "Hey, Kathleen!" he greeted, then hopped down the steps and reached his hand out to help her from the buggy. "Yeah, it's been really busy today," he replied in a playful tone. "You just missed the crowd." He smiled. "Thought I'd take a break to enjoy the nice, cool breeze. What are you two up to?"

Kathleen reached up and gave her brother a tight hug. "Well, we came to see you, dear brother!" she played.

Joshua hugged her back. "That's great! I'm happy to see you!" He kissed her on the cheek.

Martin began to tell him of the birth of the foal as Kathleen went into the store to check the latest fashions and see if any new styles of dresses or hats had arrived. On the ranch, Kathleen felt more comfortable wearing pants, like the men, but there were occasions when she liked to don a fancy dress. She was a beautiful young girl of 19, with a tiny, petite frame, but she had all the alluring gentle curves of a grown woman. Thick, wavy auburn hair grew down to the small of her back, and her green eyes glistened with hundreds of tiny flecks of gold. Delicate, full lips formed the sweet smile on her face, and the random freckles that dotted her naturally rosy cheeks completed the image and made her one of the most loved and admired citizens of Augusta.

After Martin had gone on his way, Joshua went and joined his sister inside, and the two of them sat down for a visit while they enjoyed a nice cold glass of lemonade.

Chapter 2

Southeast Nebraska Territory

As Alexander Johnson sat on the edge of his bed, he stuffed the last of his clothes into his travel bag. He knew how much his aunt and uncle hated to see him go, but he was young and restless. He was twenty-three and ready, as well as eager, to get out and start a life of his own. He had heard talk of work in the Northwest, as many men were needed to help with the never-ending construction of the railroad. When he was a small boy, he used to dream of riding with the United States Cavalry, and it was still on his mind, but Alex would look at other opportunities before he would sign up and make such a commitment. Lost in thought, he didn't hear the summons at the door. It was his uncle who knocked.

"Alex? Are you alright?" he asked.

"Huh?" Alex turned to him with a start. "Yeah, I'm fine. I'm just thinking." He let out a heavy sigh, then rose to open the door for Marcus.

"Sorry to disturb you." He pointed his thumb behind him. "Aunt Rose sent me in here to fetch ya for breakfast. She cooked up lots of good food to fill that stomach of yours before you get going. Best not let her down."

"Great!" Alex replied with a smile. "I'll be right there."

Marcus nodded and pulled the door closed again.

Alex scanned the room one last time to make sure he had packed all that he would need on his journey, then left to go eat with his family.

The table was filled with sliced ham, fresh-baked biscuits, boiled eggs, and fried potatoes. As Alex scooted his chair up to the table, he thanked Aunt Rose. "This is great! I'm starving." He smiled as they all joined hands to say grace.

"Now you eat up, Alex," Rose told him as she began to fill his plate. "You're going to need a lot of energy for your long ride."

"Thank you, Aunt Rose," Alex said as he took his heaping plate from her. "I'll eat all I can." He winked as he shoved the first forkful into his mouth.

They all ate in silence, each of them lost in their own thoughts about Alex's decision to leave. Marcus was sad to see him go, yet a little excited, as he knew his nephew could be headed for some big adventures. Rose was scared for his safety. He was still a young boy to her, and she was not yet ready to say goodbye. She fought hard to hold back the tears that stung her eyes.

Alex, on the other hand, was filled with many emotions, which ranged from anxiety and fear of the unknown to joy and excitement about what experiences lay in store for him. He couldn't wait to see the open frontier and meet new people along the way. He also hoped to see herds of buffalo and other wild creatures, and even though he was told that most of the Indians were out of these territories by now, he kept faith in the possibility of seeing some of those, as well.

The desire to leave on such a journey had prodded at him for several years, but he remained at home, for he knew it would break his aunt's heart if he were to leave. But now, it was time to go. He had to get out and live his dream to travel and explore. He promised to keep in touch by mail and that he would come home to visit at least once a year. This eased Rose's mind a little bit. She knew that every young man needed to have an adventure if they wanted one, and she didn't intend to hold him back. Silently, though, she prayed that he would fulfill his adventurous desires and return home in the next year, to stay.

When the meal was finished, Alex excused himself from the table and returned to his room to get his things. Rose began to clear away the dirty dishes, and Marcus headed out to the barn to ready Alex's horse. After the saddle was on, he filled some bags with oats and apples for him, then went to the well to fill several canteens with fresh cold water.

Saddlebags in one hand, his bedroll and travel bag in the other, Alex came out of the house and walked to the barnyard. "You don't have to do that, Uncle Marcus."

"I know, son. I want to." Then he reached into his pocket, pulled out a small leather pouch, and handed it to Alex. "Here," he said. "Open it," he coaxed when he noticed the puzzled expression on Alex's face.

Alex poured the contents into his hand. Inside were several fifty-dollar gold pieces and lots of smaller change. Still confused, Alex asked, "What's this for?"

"Well, it's for you," Marcus answered as he pushed Alex's hand away when he tried to give the money back to him. "It's yours."

"No, I can't accept this," Alex said, and tried once again to give it back. "I have been saving money for years. You keep that for yourself and Aunt Rose."

"Son, this is your money. Aunt Rose and I have been saving it for you ever since your parents died and you came to live with us. We planned to give it to you when you were grown, to help you get started on your own." He let out a downhearted chuckle, then continued, "However, we had planned on it going toward the purchase of a farm for you and a new bride," he said as he wiped a tear from his eye before it fell, "but this is your decision, and we respect it."

Alex looked down at the money in his hand, and with moist eyes, he looked back up at his uncle. "Thank you," he sniffed. "For everything." He wiped his tears with his sleeve, then gave his uncle a tight hug.

Marcus returned the strong embrace. "We are really going to miss you around here, son."

By now, Aunt Rose had joined them; her tears fell, uncontrolled. She nodded in agreement with her husband as she handed Alex a bundle that contained food for his travels. She found it difficult to speak, but was able to force a fake smile when she went to him with open arms. As she hugged him tight, and between choking sobs, she managed to say, "Be careful, son. Come home soon." She placed a loving hand on his cheek and added, "You know we love you very much."

Alex wiped away the stream of tears that ran down her cheeks. "I know, Aunt Rose. I love you both very much." He smiled as he assured her, "I'll keep in touch. And before you know it, I'll be back to see you."

"You be sure and do that," Marcus chimed in. "You know you are always welcome to come back. This will always be your home." He smiled.

Tears stung Alex's eyes, and though his dry throat felt tight and it was hard for him to speak, but he managed a simple reply. "I know." He nodded, and with that, Alex turned, walked to his horse, and mounted. He gave them one last smile, blew his aunt a kiss, then turned and rode away.

Aunt Rose walked back to the house and stood on the porch. As she put her hands over her face and silently continued to cry, she realized she may never see her nephew again. Marcus walked to her and embraced her, and as they stood together, they watched Alex as he disappeared over the hill.

Hours went by before Alex came upon a small stream where he decided to stop and let his horse rest and drink. He washed off some of the dust that clung to his hands and face, then sat down to eat some of the food that his aunt had prepared for him. He rested for a short time longer, then placed his hat on his head, checked the sun for direction, mounted his horse, and said to him, "Come on, Banjo. We've got a long way to go. We best be moving on."

Alex rode all that day, avoiding any farms, towns, or even other travelers that he happened to see in the distance. He wanted to be alone this first day and enjoy his solitude and the experience it brought with it. Alone, he felt a sense of brotherhood with nature and with the animals he saw. Jackrabbits hopped away from his path, and a small herd of deer stopped grazing long enough to watch in curiosity as he passed by. He even caught a glimpse of a frightened fox just before it ducked under a bush to hide. The wilderness was a beautiful place, he concluded, with its tall, lush prairie grass and rolling hills. As the light breeze blew through the grass, it gently swayed in perfect synchronicity, as a ripple in a pond when a stone is tossed into it. *The trees out here seem to grow taller*, he thought to himself as he passed under one and looked up into its long, densely-leafed branches. The creeks that cut their ways through these valleys bubbled more calmly than the ones he'd come across closer to home. He was in awe as he took in his beautiful surroundings, and he couldn't help but regret that he hadn't left home a year or two sooner. "Well," he said aloud to himself, "I'm here now. And I'm going to see and experience all I can." Just then, Banjo let out a nicker. Alex laughed and gave him a pat on the side of his neck. "That's right, boy. You, too!"

The day seemed to fly by, and the darkness of evening came fast. When he came upon another small stream, Alex decided it would be a good place to settle in for the night. He dismounted and removed the horse's saddle and his bedroll. He had gone on many cattle roundups and drives with his uncle, and he was used to sleeping without the luxuries of a soft down mattress and pillow. He expertly made up his bed and built a small fire that would help to protect him from curious and foraging wildlife. It would also provide warmth on this quickly chilling spring night. The smells in the air and the sounds of the nocturnal creatures were his lullabies, and they soothed him to a fast and peaceful slumber.

In the morning, Alex awoke to the bright sunshine and the sounds of birds as they sang and bullfrogs that croaked where they hid on the banks of the nearby stream. He stretched and rubbed the sleep out of his eyes, then rose and cleaned up his campsite. After he refilled his canteens from the cool stream, he grabbed a couple of strips of jerky and a hard-boiled egg for his breakfast. Then he packed up his horse and climbed up.

A click of his tongue was his travel companion's signal to go, and slowly, they continued their journey on their path toward the unknown.

As the days passed and Alex saw fewer towns and hardly any farms, he began to wonder if he had ventured too far west. Then, one day, he saw a sign of human life. Several streams of smoke rose up above the rolling hills ahead, and with them came a chilling thought. If these streams came from the fires of a native village, he could run into some trouble. Soon, his suspicions were confirmed, and he found himself surrounded by five magnificent-looking warriors on horseback.

For a moment, he felt fear like he had never felt before, but it soon dissolved when one of the men raised his hand in a friendly gesture. The others gathered and stopped a short distance away, and then the first warrior spoke. "We are of the Shoshone people," he said in near perfect English, which took Alex by complete surprise. "I am Thunder Horse." He was an impressive-looking man, and he appeared to have an important role in his tribe. A single red feather hung from a small braid on the left side of his head, and a yellow line of paint ran from the middle of his forehead straight down the center of his face to just under his chin. The claws of a mountain lion were threaded on a leather strap worn around his neck and laid against his muscular, bare chest. His pants and shoes were made from deerskin. He proudly held a staff decorated with more feathers, which Alex assumed were from an eagle. His bronze skin seemed to reflect like gold in the sunshine, and his muscles bulged in response to even his slightest movements.

Alex held up his hand to return the friendly gesture, then replied, "I am Alexander Johnson from Dodge City, Kansas." He tried to keep calm as he waited for the natives to respond. They spoke among themselves in their own language, then Thunder Horse spoke again.

"Why do you come here, Alexander Johnson?" he asked him. "Do you come alone?"

They all stared at him and awaited a response.

Alex's anxiety returned, but the calmness of his voice didn't give it away to the natives. "I am alone," he assured them. "I am traveling to visit my friends." He was uneasy about telling these people the whole truth about the reasons for his travels because of rumors he had heard, of wars between natives and the railroad companies.

Thunder Horse let out a humming moan. "You are a brave man, Alexander Johnson," he stated. He studied Alex carefully as he drew near. "You have only one rifle," he observed. He guided his horse to circle Alex's as he continued to inspect who he undoubtedly perceived as an intruder. He spoke to the other men and they laughed, but grew still again when Thunder Horse raised his hand to silence them. Alex grew more uneasy, but he sat high in the saddle and continued to face forward as the man touched his belongings and slightly taunted him.

Thunder Horse turned his horse to stop just next to Alex's, so close that the two men's knees touched as they faced each other.

The proud warrior leaned in closer to look deep into Alex's eyes, and his expression changed from soft playfulness to a cold, hard stare. He asked, "What would you do, Alexander Johnson, if I were to raise my knife to you?" His hand quickly went to the bone handle of a knife that was sheathed to his waistband.

As Alex turned his gaze to look into the eyes of Thunder Horse, he replied, "I did not come here to fight with you. I am a traveler, not a warrior. I only wish to pass by in peace." Alex could see the eyes of his challenger grow soft as he spoke, and he felt a rush of relief invade his body.

With eyes still locked, Thunder Horse spoke again to his fellow braves, and they all turned and rode away. Then he replied to Alex, "I will ride with you to the border of our land."

Alex nodded. "Thank you, Thunder Horse."

They rode along in silence for quite a while before Thunder Horse spoke out of curiosity. "Do you know it is not safe for a white man to ride alone through these lands? Do you have no fear?"

Alex smiled at his companion, and as he felt a bit more relaxed now, he replied, "Yes, I have fear. But I am a peaceful man, and I believe that there is peace and goodness in every other man as well."

The brave was confused. "There is peace and goodness in a lone man, but not always when there is more than one together." He paused and watched to see if Alex's expression changed. It didn't. "Has no one told you of the wars between the natives and the white man?" Alex nodded. Thunder Horse let out another moan. "It is good that you come to our lands, Alexander Johnson, and not the lands of another people," he lectured him. "We have lived near the white people, and we trade in their villages. We have learned that there are good whites and there are bad whites, but many of our enemies have not known the good ones, only the bad." He stopped Alex as he continued to talk. "There are many nations who only know the white man as the enemy." He extended his arm toward the southern horizon. "If you lose your way and go too far, they will find you first, as we did two days ago." He looked at a mystified Alex, then added, "And they will not want to talk."

As he took in everything that the other man had told him, Alex remained calm. "Thank you, Thunder Horse. I will be careful." They continued their ride in silence.

In the distance to his right, Alex could see many tall, cone-shaped structures that he decided, must be tepees, the homes of these people that he had heard of. He saw children playing games and some young boys racing on painted ponies. Other people were busy with chores, and there were others who stood still, looking at him in wonder. Alex broke the silence. "Do you have a wife?" he asked.

Thunder Horse looked at him for a short time then responded with a stern, "No." He became silent again.

Alex found it difficult to keep still, for it had been many days since he had left home and had the company of another person. "Are you a chief?"

"Why do you ask me these questions, Alexander Johnson?" Thunder Horse seemed a little mystified by his friendliness. Then he looked at Alex and remembered he could relax. He let out a chuckle, then replied, "No, I am not a chief. I am a protector of our people." He looked at Alex again. "That is why I am the one who came to you before you got too close to our village." He raised his hand and, in one motion, swept the countryside and continued, "I watch over our land to keep it safe for our leaders, for my people and for our children." His voice was very proud.

Alex let out a chuckle. "You do a good job, Thunder Horse." He smiled. "I was very frightened when you approached me."

"No, Alexander Johnson," the native replied. "You had little fear. Men fight when they have fear." There was a pause. "Never before have I seen a man as brave as you."

Pride filled Alex's heart when he heard these words come from one of the most courageous man he had ever met. The rest of the ride was silent as Alex pondered their conversations and the events that transpired in the past few hours. It wasn't much longer until they came to a wide, lazy river where Thunder Horse stopped his horse.

"This is where we must part, Alexander Johnson." He motioned to the river. "This is the best place to cross. If you stay on this path, you will be safe all the way to your people."

Alex extended his hand and replied, "Please, call me Alex." As he held his hand steady and offered his friendship. Thunder Horse just stared at it for a while and held his ground. After a time, Alex felt that he may have misinterpreted his companion's intentions. He had believed that the accompaniment was for his guidance and maybe for his protection. Now, it dawned on him that perhaps Thunder Horse rode with him because he didn't trust him. It was possible he had escorted him out of the area to benefit his people and to protect his own family. He tried again. "I'm one of the good ones," he said with a friendly, reassuring smile.

Thunder Horse knew what the gesture meant in the white man's culture, but he had never expected that it would be given to him. He also never expected to want so badly to accept such an offer. He did, and as he took Alex's hand, they held their eyes fixed on each other's. "Yes, I know." He relaxed again.

"Thank you, my friend." Alex smiled. "I will never forget you."

Thunder Horse let out a sort of grunt and gave a nod of agreement as he pulled his hand away. "Go now. I will watch you cross the river."

Alex nodded, then turned Banjo around. The horse stepped carefully on the rocky bed, keeping his balance as the water rushed around them. The current was swift, but the river was shallow enough that crossing was easy. By the time they made it to the other side, Alex turned to give one last wave. The brave was gone. It was almost as if he had never been there to begin with. Alex shrugged, and they turned and continued on their way.

Chapter 3

The city council meeting had just come to a close and Martin and Joshua were both members. Joshua returned to the store where Kathleen had been working for him. "Hey, beautiful," he greeted her when he walked in the door.

"Hi, Joshua." She greeted him with a smile. "How did the meeting go?"

Her brother shrugged. "Oh, you know. Same old stuff." He stepped behind the counter and told her that their father would be back shortly. "He had some business to do at the bank, but he said it wouldn't take long."

"That's alright," Kathleen replied as she walked toward the door. "I'll go out and wait on the steps. It's a bit stuffy in here." As she reached for the knob to open the door, a dusty, weather-beaten young man opened it from the other side. His appearance was rugged with his shirt torn and tattered. Dust covered his pants and his boots were scuffed so thin that his toes were almost through the leather. More trail dust hid the color of his shoulder-length hair, and his beard was long and bushy. Whiskers hid most of his face, but she could see the gentleness in the dark eyes peeked that through the grime on his face. His shoulders were broad and his chest appeared to be muscular, with a tuft of dust-covered dark hair that peeked out above the shreds of what used to be a shirt. But even through all that filth, his attractive features showed, and that made it difficult for Kathleen to pull her eyes away.

He, too, was in awe at the radiance he saw before him. Kathleen soon gathered her wits, and she raised her hand quickly to her mouth to suppress a gasp of surprise. Their eyes met and locked until she came fully to her senses, then shyly turned away.

"After you, miss." He removed his hat and bowed slightly while he held the door for her. He couldn't pull his gaze from her face.

Timidly, she smiled and pardoned herself, then she grabbed up a bit of her skirt, turned sideways, and quickly passed through the open doorway. Outside, she saw the good sheriff, and she greeted him happily. "Good morning, Sheriff Taylor." She was now able to relax a bit. "Lovely day, isn't it?" She tried to ignore the strange man who accompanied him, but found it difficult, as she could still feel his eyes upon her while she spoke.

"Yes it is, Kathleen." He smiled cheerfully. "Just saw your daddy," he added as he tipped his hat back off his forehead and wiped the sweat from his brow. "How's everything out at the ranch?" The sheriff was a heavy man with a belly that bulged out and hung over his gun belt. Big bushy eyebrows matched his thick gray mustache, and the spectacles he wore almost always sat at the end of his round, red nose. He was a happy man, and people could hear it in his voice as it sang out when he greeted them on the street.

"Everything is just fine, thank you," she replied. "How are Mrs. Taylor and the children?"

They continued to talk about this and that, but Alex didn't hear another word. He became hypnotized by her beauty as he watched every movement and facial expression she made. He carefully studied her and memorized every striking detail. Her lips had the perfect fullness for kissing, and her smile exposed delicate little dimples that were otherwise hidden. Her nose was turned up slightly, and it moved a little with each word she spoke.

The gold flecks in her eyes showed her gentle nature, and when a slight breeze caught hold of some strands of her long, auburn hair, she tucked it away behind tiny, delicate ears.

He became bold as he nervously continued his furtive quest and moved his eyes lower. He noticed that her dress was the same light green that he found in her eyes. Her hands were tiny, with dainty fingernails. The buttons on her sleeves were a darker green than that of the dress and they matched the ribbons in her hair. It took all the strength he had to look away from her when he faintly heard the sheriff say his name.

"Alexander Johnson, I'd like you to meet Kathleen Sheldon."

His hat was already removed, so Alex presented his hand, momentarily forgetting how dirty it was. She hesitated when she looked down at it, but with a polite smile, she began to extend her hand to him as well. But before she could kindly take his hand into her petite, spotless one, he quickly retracted it. "Oh!" he pardoned himself. "Perhaps after I've cleaned up a bit." He let out a nervous chuckle.

"Yes," Kathleen replied, with a slight giggle and a polite curtsy. "Perhaps." She looked out into the street, then added, "Oh, there's my daddy." She pointed out into the traffic to the buggy as it neared, then she excused herself. "It was a pleasure," she said, and turned as she opened her parasol before she descended down the steps to the street.

"Good day, Kathleen," the sheriff replied.

"Good day, ma'am," Alex called to her.

Sheriff Taylor turned to Alex and, with a mocking tone, he jested, "Not too good with the ladies, hey, young fella?" He let out a bellowing laugh as passed by him and went into the store.

"Was that an angel?" Alex asked, dumbfounded, as he looked at the buggy as if it were a chariot that carried away the princess. After it melted into the traffic's dust and disappeared from sight, he turned reluctantly and followed the sheriff inside.

Joshua greeted them, and the sheriff introduced Alex. "Alex just got into town this morning. He's been traveling for several weeks on horseback."

Joshua was impressed. "Wow! That must have been quite a journey," he exclaimed. "You're lucky you made it here alive."

Alex let out a loud sigh. "Yeah," he replied. "Someday, I'll tell ya about it. It was quite an adventure!" His encounter with Thunder Horse never left his thoughts, nor did the spiritual feelings it gave him. He wasn't sure if this was a story to share, though, so he decided to keep it to himself and treasure the memory.

"I'd like that." Joshua smiled. "I'm always up for a good story!" When he patted him on the shoulder, he sent up a little dust and playfully waved it away, then chuckled as he pointed in the direction of the clothing. Alex walked toward the back of the store; another customer entered, and the sheriff said goodbye then took his leave.

Joshua helped the patron and Alex did his shopping. He found himself some new garments and boots then went to the counter to pay. He and Joshua spent over an hour, talking, and through there many topics of conversations, Alex found out that Joshua was Kathleen's brother. After he watched his facial expressions as he spoke and noticed the color of his eyes, he saw the remarkable resemblance.

When Joshua learned that Alex had decided to stay in Augusta for a while and take a rest from his travels, and that he would be looking for work, Joshua could tell by his demeanor that he was a good and honest man. He told Alex that he had been thinking about hiring help, and that if he was interested, the job was his and that he could start that very afternoon. Alex gladly accepted.

"Great!" Joshua said, then added, "Be here at three o'clock. I've got orders for some goods that we can start loading up tonight and deliver first thing in the morning."

Alex smiled. "That sounds real good! I'll be here." They parted with a handshake, and

Alex took his purchase and left to go and find a tub of nice warm bathwater at the hotel that Joshua had recommended.

～

When Kathleen and Martin stopped in front of the steps of the house, Hattie, the head maid, was out on the front porch to greet them. She had a picnic basket in one hand and a bundled blanket in the other. "Hungry?" she asked them.

"Hattie, you are the best!" Martin cheered, then hopped down from the buggy and took her arm to help her up into it.

They drove a few miles from the house to a hill that overlooked their ranch to the west. From there, they had a beautiful view of the mountain range that divided the territories.

This was their favorite picnic spot. There was an old oak tree near the top of the hill that provided dense, cool shade, and that is where they spread the blanket while Hattie began to unpack the basket.

Hattie came to live with the Sheldons just before Kathleen was born. She was hired to be a maid, but when Anna began to fall ill, she became Kathleen's nanny. They formed a very special bond, and when Kathleen's mother died, that bond became even stronger.

Hattie was like a second mother to her. Later, when Kathleen was old enough and didn't need a nanny anymore, Martin offered her a position as overseer of the house workers, which she gladly accepted, for she knew it would have broken her heart to have to leave this family. She had felt at home here since the day she arrived, over eighteen years ago.

As they ate their chicken and biscuits, they casually chatted about events of their day and the upcoming festival that Augusta had every year in late July. They reminisced about past festivals and expressed their individual wonders about what this year's celebration had in store for the town. As they chatted, Kathleen's mind wandered to the stranger, Alexander, that she had met in town today. The thought of him, covered with travel dust, made her curious to know what he really looked like under all that filth. She just knew he was very handsome, and she prayed that he wasn't some drifter that'd be gone in the morning, because she wanted to find out if her instincts were correct. His eyes looked gentle; his smile was genuine. He just had to be handsome. She smiled to herself at the thought.

When they finished eating and everything was back in the basket, they sat and enjoyed the view for a while longer. Martin lit his pipe, and they talked about anything that came to mind. Before long, though, they realized the sun had made its way down to the hilltops on the horizon and the air had grown a bit cooler. The view and the gentle breeze were relaxing after a hot and busy afternoon, but they knew their day wasn't over yet. There were still some chores to be done, inside the house and out in the stables. It was time to go.

Martin rose, and during a long stretch, he asked them, "Are you two beautiful ladies ready to go? It's going to be dark soon."

"Don't make me laugh with that beautiful stuff," Hattie snarled as she struggled to get up from her place on the blanket.

Martin grabbed her and lifted her with ease, then began to dance around with her in his arms. After he told her again and again that she was beautiful, he let her down and laid a loud smacking kiss on her plump, rosy cheek.

Hattie let out a scream. "You crazy fool!" she said, and continued to mumble to herself as she swayed dizzily back toward the buggy. Martin and Kathleen laughed as they followed close behind.

Alex checked into a room at the hotel and was getting ready for his bath when he glanced into the mirror that hung on the wall. For the first time, he saw how bad he looked. "Damn, you're a mess!" he muttered to his reflection with a sneer. "Kathleen must think I'm an awful pig." Then a smile formed and he decided that, after he was cleaned up, he'd see to it that they met again. He would charm her in any way he could think to win her heart. He closed his eyes and smiled to himself as he remembered her pretty face and the golden twinkle in her fawn-like eyes.

As he sank slowly into the tub, the clean, hot water made him moan as every muscle in his body began to relax. He realized that he had almost forgotten what it felt like to be clean. While he soaked, he thought of things he could do to kill some time before three o'clock. He needed to write Uncle Marcus and Aunt Rose a letter and let them know where he was and that he was safe and settled here for the time being. That should bring them some comfort, for he knew that they were probably very worried about him. He also knew that Aunt Rose could not get a proper night's sleep when she was worried about something. He was pretty sure she hadn't slept nary a wink since he left home.

After he soaked a while, he finished his bath, then trimmed his beard and mustache to the length that he liked. As he got dressed, he realized he didn't remember a time that it felt so good to put on nice, clean clothes. He glanced into the mirror one last time to ensure he was presentable enough for the public, congratulated himself on a job well done, and went out to explore the town.

Along the wood-planked sidewalks, Alex greeted friendly people with smiles and hellos.

He looked into the widows of shops, and once in a while, he stopped to chat with a gentleman who introduced himself. At the church, he visited with the reverend, who welcomed him to town and invited him to attend the service on Sunday. The post office had paper and envelopes, so he jotted a quick note to his family and sent it right away. At exactly three o'clock, Alex was at the store to meet up with Joshua and start his new job.

Joshua had just finished a transaction with a customer when Alex walked through the door. When he looked at him, he instantly knew who Alex was, but couldn't help but tease him a little. He stared at him as if in utter disbelief. "Alex?" he asked as he slowly stepped out from behind the counter and approached him. "Is that you?"

"Very funny!" Alex laughed with him as he reached up and stroked his clean face. "I know. I looked pretty bad, didn't I?"

"I hardly recognized you!" Joshua laughed. "I know what it's like, though. I've been on quite a few cattle drives where I came home and looked just as bad, if not worse." Joshua thought back to those days for a moment, then added, "Kind of nice, though, isn't it? Getting away from it all, seeing the frontier and not giving a care about how you look or how you smell."

Alex nodded in agreement. "I loved every minute of my travels here. There is a lot of beautiful land out there, but honestly, I never laid my eyes on anything is as beautiful as the sight I saw in here this morning." He pointed toward the door where he had first seen Kathleen.

Joshua smiled, as he knew that Alex referred to his sister. "Yeah, well," he told him, "if you're ready to get to work, we have some flour, ice, and milk to deliver, and some of it goes out to my father's ranch." He winked at Alex. Then he took off his apron and added, "But first, I'm hungry! How about a big juicy steak." He threw the apron on the counter, put his hand on Alex's shoulder, and added, "And then I'm going to buy you a beer." Alex thanked him for the offer, and they went out the door and across the street to Bonnie's Eating House.

When they finished their meal, they found the town less active, for most of the people had gone home to retire for the evening. Where the day noises of buggies, horses' whinnies and people's voices once flooded the streets, piano music, clanging glasses, and men's laughter now took over. Once inside the large, smoke-filled room of Merle's Saloon, they scanned the scene. A few men stood at the bar that stretched most of the length of the room, and several tables were scattered throughout the establishment, their chairs occupied by groups of men as they played cards or just visited and relaxed after a long, hot day of work. Cut tree trunks served as pillars throughout, to support and hold up the ceiling. In a corner of the room, a tall lanky man wearing a red-and-white pinstriped shirt and matching top hat played the piano. Bottles of whiskey filled the shelves behind the bar and partially covered the large dusty mirror behind them.

As they walked through the room toward the bar, Joshua was greeted by several townspeople who knew him. He briefly introduced Alex, and they continued on. Once at the bar, they ordered two beers from Sam, the bartender.

Before he took a drink, Alex lifted his mug to Joshua in gesture to thank him, and just as he put the glass to his lips, one of the working girls walked from across the room and stood beside him at the bar. "Hey there, good looking," she said as she looked him over, top to bottom. "Buy me a drink?"

Joshua chuckled at him teasingly, but Alex was too polite to refuse. "Sure," he motioned toward the bartender. "What would you like?"

"Gimme a whiskey, Sam," she ordered, then turned back to Alex. As she lit a cigarette, she looked him over again. "What's your name, cowboy?" she asked, then took a long drag from her cigarette and blew the smoke from the corner of her mouth.

Joshua nudged him from behind and laughed again; this time, it caused Alex to smile, but he contained a snicker so as not to appear to be rude. "Alex," he replied as he touched the brim of his hat. "What's yours?"

"Men call me Sunshine," she replied, then she took another drag from her cigarette, and as she ran her tongue suggestively along her top lip, the smoke escaped and rose toward the ceiling to blend with the thick cloud that already hung there.

Politely, he replied, "Hello, Sunshine. How do you do?"

She smiled, then leaned into him and whispered, "Very well, so I'm told." She reached out to fondle the hair that taunted her from the collar of his shirt, but then Joshua grabbed his buddy and pulled him away.

"Our chairs are open!" he told Alex, then nodded toward the poker tables. "Let's go get in the game."

Relieved, Alex agreed, and they walked away and left Sunshine alone to pout until she found another victim to try and seduce for her whiskey. "Thanks!" he whispered as they walked away. "I wasn't sure how I was going to get myself out of that one." Then he added, "It was almost scarier than..." He stopped himself. He had almost spoken of his encounter with the Indians, and though his comment was sincere, he couldn't say it.

"Than what?" Joshua asked.

"Never mind." He brushed off the conversation and walked to the table. Joshua shrugged, then followed and let it drop.

Chapter 4

Martin, Kathleen, and Hattie chatted cheerfully as they drove home in the darkening skies of twilight, but as they rounded the hill and turned into the tree-lined lane that led to their house, they saw the terrifying sight of their beautiful home ablaze.

Martin rose slowly in disbelief. "Dear God!" he exclaimed, and as he faltered in shock.

He slowly climbed down from the wagon, unable to look away. "My dear God!" he repeated and gasped. "Our home! Kathleen," he spoke rather calmly, "go and get Joshua." And without hesitation, he was running toward the house.

As Kathleen took the reins, Hattie climbed out of the wagon and began to follow Martin, but suddenly, fear forced her to stop in her tracks. In the distance, in the dim light of the rising full moon, she could barely make out the silhouettes of men as they ran into the grove of trees beyond the house yard.

Kathleen had driven the wagon before, but never so hard or fast as she did now. As tears welled up in her eyes and her hair whipped around her face, her vision was nil. She prayed the horse could find her way as Kathleen slapped her again and again with the reins and begged her to go faster. Visions ran through her mind. She pictured her bedroom, the library, her father's den, and the other beautifully decorated rooms. These were just some of the many attributes that her mother left behind for the family to enjoy and visitors to admire. Now burning. All that would be left was black ash to cover what once was painted walls and cherry wood upholstered furniture. Memories rose of when she looked through catalogs with her mother to help her choose which drapes and rugs they wanted to order. She remembered the day that her father and five other men carried in the piano that was ordered from New Jersey. Hattie and her mother had stood on chairs as they hung the pictures on the walls, and she herself had helped her mother paint the white pillars on the front porch.

She cried even harder, knowing how her father must be feeling. The house was all he had left of his wife. The love that she put into it and all of the wonderful memories of her were in the home that they had made together.

After what seemed to be hours, Kathleen finally got to the town. She went straight to the mercantile, but found it dark. Quickly, she jumped out of the wagon and ran around to the back to see if the delivery wagon was there. Maybe Joshua was still out making deliveries. She found the wagon loaded and ready to go, but her brother wasn't there.

Then it dawned on her. There was another place he may be. She ran down the street and around the corner, and when she got to the saloon, she ran up the steps and through the doors. Breathless, she stood in the doorway and scanned the room. Most of the men inside looked up from what they were doing and stared at her.

Joshua stood from a table near the back and ran to her the moment he saw her. Relieved, she began to cry again. "Joshua! Thank God I found you!" She lost all strength in her legs when his arms went around her. She hugged him tightly as she sobbed into his chest.

"Kathleen," he said as he held her tight. "What happened?"

Between sobs, she choked out, "Our house... is... on fire!"

Joshua scooped her up into his arms and carried her to the first wagon he came to. He and Alex climbed in on either side. Many of the other men left the saloon too and mounted their horses or climbed into their wagons and headed at top speed toward the Sheldon ranch. Alex held Kathleen and comforted her all the way. To her, the ride home seemed to take longer than the ride to town, and once they arrived, they could see there was no way that they could save the house or anything in it.

When Hattie saw them, she ran to greet them, and when Joshua jumped out of the wagon, she grabbed him. Her face was streaked with dirt and tears and her voice was shaky, but she managed to say to him, "Mr. Sheldon, your daddy is in there!"

Alex looked toward the house, then glanced back to Joshua and Kathleen. He saw the horrified expressions on their faces. Memories flooded his mind. He heard his mother's screams and his father's calls for help.

The sound of the window glass as it broke and the deafening roar of the flames helped him to decide that he had no other choice. He ran toward the house as fast as he could, with Joshua right behind him. Just as Alex reached for the door, Joshua grabbed his arm. "No!" he cried. "You can't go in there!"

"Let me go, Joshua!" Alex hollered back over the roar of the flames as he pulled his arm free. "I have to try!" He opened the door and went inside.

The smoke stung in his eyes, so he knelt to the floor and began to look around. Flames crawled up the walls, and thick, dark smoke hid the high ceilings. Once again, his mind took him back to where he had sat in the grass and watched as his own family's home burn to the ground, so many years ago. He shook his head to clear it, and as he crawled along, he looked for any signs of life. The heat made him dizzy, and he coughed on the smoke that began to fill his lungs. He searched aimlessly for a hand or a foot or anything that resembled a body. Suddenly, he heard the sound of the wood as it creaked above his head. When he looked up, he caught sight of a man as he began to descend the blazing staircase. In his arms, he carried a large oil painting. "Mr.

Sheldon!" he called to him, but as soon as Alex stood to go to him, the steps gave way and Martin fell through.

The roar of the flames was deafening, but Alex yelled his name again and again, hoping Martin would hear him and reply. Once again, he got down on his knees, and as he crawled toward the staircase, he saw what appeared to be a closet door under the steps. He pulled it open and found Martin struggling to free himself from the burning wood that pinned him down. "Help me!" Martin pleaded as he reached a hand to Alex.

Alex stood and grabbed Martin's hand, then pulled him out of the closet and out from under the burning piece of wood. He removed his shirt and wrapped it around Martin's legs, then lifted him to carry him out of the house. As he found his way to the door, he could hear the half-conscious and delirious man mumble, repeating the same words over and over again.

Huddled together, Joshua and Kathleen stood and watched as the house burned. They wondered if they would ever see their beloved father or Alex again. Just then, the two men burst from the house, stumbled down the steps, and fell in the grass in front of them.

Kathleen pulled herself from her brother's arms and ran to her father's side. He was unconscious. "Is he dead?" she asked in a shaky voice. Tears streamed down her face as she reached out to touch him.

"No," Alex choked. "He's alive." He stepped back and coughed, then spit the soot from his mouth. Exhausted, he breathed heavily to pull in some clean, fresh air, and once he was able to stand, he looked at them through squinted and burning eyes and asked, "Who's Anna?"

The siblings looked at each other, then looked at him in bewilderment. Her eyes fell to the ground and in a tone filled with forlorn, Kathleen replied, "She was our mother."

Just then, Alex regained all his strength and energy and darted back toward the door. He remembered the painting that Martin had in his arms. It was of a woman whom he instantly assumed was Anna. He hesitated briefly at the door before he reentered. Joshua and Kathleen looked at each other in fear as Joshua staggered slowly toward the porch, staring after Alex in disbelief. In less than a minute, Alex returned. He coughed and choked again, this time carrying the portrait.

"Are you crazy?" Joshua demanded as he grabbed Alex and spun him around to face him. "You could have been killed in there."

When Alex caught his breath again and was able to speak, he explained to Joshua that his father was carrying the portrait when he found him. "I figured, since he risked his own life to go in and get it in the first place, it must be something very special to him." After he took a few more deep, refreshing breaths, he added in a calmer, clearer, and more serious manner, "I don't think he wants to lose his wife all over again."

Kathleen stood up and went to Alex. She wrapped her arms around him and gave him a strong, tight hug that Alex returned. He comfortingly patted her on the back until she pulled away and looked into his eyes. When he wiped a tear from her face, she came to realize who this stranger was, and she smiled. "Thank you, Mr. Johnson."

"Please, it's Alex." He smiled. "And you're welcome."

Joshua extended his gratitude as well and told him he was a blessing. Alex laughed. "No, Joshua. I'm your friend."

When Martin awoke briefly, the siblings knelt by his side to comfort him, and Alex decided that this was his chance to slip away. He felt good about what he had done, but he didn't want to be thanked for it. He did it for himself, as well as for them, to help him rid himself of the guilt he carried for his own parents' deaths. He knew that it wasn't his fault that he couldn't save them, for he was just a child when they died, but the visions had haunted him all of his life. He hoped now, with this act of courage, he could put them to rest and feel better about himself.

The townsmen who came to help, now stood around them. "We're sorry, Mr. Sheldon." George Clayton was a local man who spoke first. "We tried to save some things, but the fire moved too fast." He held his hat in his hands and looked regretfully at the ground.

Hattie slowly walked towards them with a horrified look on her face. Kathleen was the first to notice her. "Hattie?" she asked as she rose from the ground to approach her. "What is it, Hattie? What's wrong?" She could tell there was more than sorrow in the woman's eyes. Something had frightened her.

Joshua took Hattie's hands in his and she looked into his eyes. She put her hand to her chest to ease the hard thuds of her heart, then stuttered out the words, "I saw the men who did this." She paused for another deep breath. Everyone was quiet as they waited for her to continue. "It was Indians, Mr. Sheldon. I saw five or six of them run into the woods behind the house. They had blankets and chickens and I don't know what else." She sighed with relief that she was able to speak, then wearily, she knelt to sit beside Kathleen on the grass.

The men looked at each other and walked away, then huddled in conversation. After a few moments, Zack Thomas spoke up. "Come on, men." He sprinted to his horse and mounted. He was soon joined by the rest of the men that had come on horseback, and he called back to Joshua. "We're going to gather more men and set out first thing in the morning to gather up your stock. We'll also see if we can find any signs of which direction the Indians went. Maybe we can put an end to this nightmare." With that, they all turned their horses and headed back to town to ready themselves for the morning's mission.

Chapter 5

Alex came to a rough wagon trail after he took his silent leave. The tracks ran along the fence line of the house's yard and went in the direction of the main road. He made sure the family members were all alright, then felt if he'd stayed any longer, he'd have been an intruder. He had a lot to deal with, himself. Thoughts of the events that led him here, thoughts of released guilt and, of course, thoughts of the sweet girl whose life had changed drastically within these last hours.

The road was rutted with an occasional rock or sage bush that caused the path to swerve a little to the left or to the right, but as the full moon rose above the treetops, his path became better lit, allowing him to see the obstacles and avoid them.

As he walked along, he allowed his thoughts to drift to Kathleen's warm embrace and her sweet smile. He longed to wipe the tears from her eyes and to hold her, to comfort her and to tell her that everything was going to be alright. He imagined what it would have been like if the circumstances were different. He would have pulled her into his arms and returned her hug. He would have raised her chin so that she would look into his eyes, then he would have leaned down to… He smiled to himself as his step got a little lighter, like he was floating on air, then thought it best to let his mind wander to other things.

It was a beautiful night, all things considered. The gentle breeze blew some clouds around in the sky above, and the smell in the air hinted at rain. Insects chirped and buzzed all around him. An owl hooted, then flew from one treetop to another. It was almost as if the tragedy at the Sheldons' ranch had never taken place. He wished that it was all just a bad dream that he'd awoken from, but he knew it was a nightmare this family would never forget.

Somewhere during his musing, he'd found the main road and now could faintly see the silhouette of the structures of town just ahead. He trudged wearily along, but when he got to his hotel, he practically ran up the steps to the second floor as he longed for the feel of the down-stuffed salvation that awaited him in his room. But when he got to the top step and rounded the banister to go down the hall, he stopped suddenly. His door was ajar, and the light from the oil lamp illuminated the room. He used caution as he peered inside, but when he found the half-naked Sunshine sprawled out on his bed, anger over-took him. He pushed the door open all the way and demanded, "What are you doing here?"

She sat up with a bit of a start then relaxed when she saw it was him. "It's about time, cowboy." Calmly, she reached over, took a cigarette off of the bedside table, and lit it. She inhaled deeply, and as she exhaled the smoke, added, "I was about to give up on you."

Growing impatient and with anger in his tone, he asked her again, "Why are you here, Sunshine, and how did you get in?"

She extinguished her cigarette in a half empty glass of water, then crawled across to the edge of the bed where he stood and got on her knees to be at his level. "I have a very tricky tongue," she laughed, then licked her lips in a seductive manner. "I've been waiting all night for this." She began to rub her hands on his bare chest, and when he raised his hands to gently push her away, she grabbed them and placed them on her breasts. "You smell like you're on fire, baby," she panted. "You been hot for me, too?" She moved her hands down to his belt and began to undo the buckle. "I give real good baths."

"No!" Alex grabbed her hands and held them away from him, then he gently pushed her away. He grabbed a clean shirt for himself, then quickly gathered up her clothes and threw them down on the bed beside her. "Get dressed, and please get out of here," he demanded, then calmly left the room and closed the door behind him.

Sunshine jumped up, ran to the door and opened it, then called out to him, "Come back, cowboy." She let out a deviant chuckle. "I promise you won't regret it!"

Feeling outraged, Alex put on his shirt as he leaped down the steps two at a time and out the door of the hotel. He went next door to the livery stable, where his horse was stabled, saddled him then quickly rode, aimlessly, toward the outskirts of town.

He rode for what seemed to be miles, until his heartbeat slowed and his adrenaline returned to normal, his weariness getting the better of him. He slowed Banjo to a walk, then guided him off the road and through a small grove of trees, hoping to find a nice place to sleep. He didn't care that he didn't have his bedroll. A nice patch of tall grass would make a perfect bed for him tonight. Then he saw it. The most placid and inviting pond he had ever seen. It lay down in a valley just beyond a property fence. The moon's light reflected beautifully upon the mirror-like surface and taunted him with the thought of a cool, refreshing moonlight swim. "It has to be well past midnight," he reasoned with Banjo. "Who will know?" He decided he'd just take a little swim to give Sunshine time to give up on him returning, hoping she'd be gone by the time he got back. He tied his horse to the fence and climbed over, then stripped his clothes off and dropped them piece by piece as he walked to the water's edge. He carefully waded into the cool, refreshing water.

The Sheldon siblings huddled together on the grass with their father as they, tearfully watched their house burn. Martin was still unconscious. Suddenly, Joshua's attention went toward the barn when he caught movement from the corner of his eye. "Tommy!" he called as he got up and ran to the boy who cautiously came out from the shadows. The traumatized twelve-year-old held out his arms to Joshua and began to cry as he curled safely into the embrace of soothing arms. Joshua lowered himself to the ground and held him as he sobbed.

The boy sniffed. "Are they gone?" he asked.

Joshua stroked his head and replied, "Yeah, they're gone." They rose and walked over to where Kathleen sat with their father, and Tommy took a seat beside her. She put a comforting arm around him just as they heard a buggy coming up the drive. It was Dr. Holbrook.

"I got here as soon as I got word, Joshua," he said as he grabbed his medical gear, jumped down, and ran to Martin's side. "How bad is he?" he asked as he knelt down and opened his bag. He pulled out some scissors to cut away the legs of Martin's pants as Joshua held up a lantern for light.

"He's been unconscious for quite some time now, Doc," Joshua replied, then regretfully admitted, "We don't know what to do for him."

The doctor nodded, and as he continued to work on his father, Joshua asked Tommy if he knew where the rest of the stable hands were. Tommy shrugged. "I dunno, Mr. Sheldon." He wiped tears from his eyes. "The last thing I remember was one of those Indians pulling Max into a stable. He was hitting him with something."

Joshua held the lantern out to Tommy who stood and took it. "Please hold this right here for Doc," he instructed, then started for the barn.

Kathleen called after him in a sort of loud whisper, "Be careful, Joshua!" who replied to her with a wave as he crept cautiously.

"Holler when you find them!" Doc called out. Hattie had gotten some water from the well to clean Martin's burns, and after the doctor gave Kathleen and Hattie a few instructions on how to clean the wounds, he decided he'd better go and assist Joshua.

The two men stood for a moment at the doorway as they peered into the darkness of the unlit barn. Joshua called to Max, and the two of them remained motionless as they listened for a response or any sounds of movement. They exchanged glances, each one terrified of what they may find. Joshua reached up to take a lantern that hung from a hook, lit it, and held it high to illuminate the shadows. Instantly, Doc Holbrook saw a man's boot peeking out from behind the wall of a stall and ran toward it. It was Max.

Joshua followed and held the lantern close so the doctor could see. Then, after a loud gulp, he gathered his courage and asked, "Is he alive?"

The doctor let out a sigh of relief and replied, "Yes, he's alive." Immediately, he began to inspect Max's wounds.

Joshua hung the lantern on a nearby nail and went to fetch another one, then took a quick look around and in the other stalls. "There's no one else in here. If you don't need my help, I'm going to take a look around outside."

Doc nodded as he continued to work. "Go!" He poured some alcohol onto a cloth and began to clean the wounds on Max's face and head.

Joshua began his search as he walked the perimeter of the barn, again holding the lantern as high as he could. As he rounded a corner, he found one of Max's helpers, Ross. He had been shot through the heart with an arrow. Joshua knelt down beside him and looked into his lifeless eyes. They seemed to gaze peacefully into the clear, starry sky above. "Rest easy now, Ross," Joshua said as he removed his shirt and covered the spiritless shell. A tear slipped from his eye.

Then, off to his left, just a few yards away from where he knelt, Joshua heard a moan. He quickly picked up the lantern and cautiously walked toward the noise to investigate. It was Robbie, Ross's younger brother.

"Mr. Sheldon," he whispered as he reached out to him, holding a bloody arrow in his hand. He too, had been shot. His wound was in his stomach. "I got the arrow out." He gave a weak, shaky smile as he held up the trophy.

"Doc!" Joshua called over his shoulder. "Over here!" He knelt down and took Robbie's hand in his. "Lie still," he soothed. "Help is on the way."

Robbie continued to smile. His voice trembled and a tear ran down his face. "I got the arrow out, Mr. Sheldon." he repeated. "That means I'm gonna be alright now, right?"

"Yes, Robbie, you're going to be fine." Joshua knew he may have just lied to him, but he wanted him to remain calm so Dr. Holbrook could see to his wounds. "Just lie still."

Just as the doctor got to them, Robbie's hand slipped from Joshua's, and he too was gone. Tears welled up in Joshua's eyes as he removed his undershirt and laid it gently over the young man's face. Doc picked up his bag, let out a heavy sigh, and turned to walk back into the barn to where Max still lay unconscious. Joshua picked up the lantern and continued around the barnyard, praying he wouldn't find any more dead men.

Sheriff Taylor arrived, and Kathleen got up to greet him. He was followed by some of the men from town who had been there earlier in the night. After giving her a comforting hug and getting the report on her daddy, he excused himself, and he and the others walked to the barn where Joshua and the doctor stood. They huddled together and spoke in voices Kathleen couldn't hear. Soon, they all got lanterns, lit them, and dispersed into various directions to search the area for whoever, or whatever, they could find.

Then, out of the shadows of the trees, from the direction of the cattle hands' cabins, approached several ladies, also carrying lanterns. They were the wives of the cattlemen. Sarah spoke to Kathleen. "Miss Sheldon," she said with condolences in her voice, "the ladies and I made up a cabin for you and your daddy, for the time being." The other ladies stepped forward. "We got clean bedding and clothes, lots of food and fresh water." She pointed to one of the other ladies. "Mary here made some stew, and we got a nice fire burning in the fireplace." She began to sob. "We didn't see what was happening up here, Miss Sheldon. We can't see the house through all the trees. We're all so sorry. We…"

Kathleen took Sarah's hands in hers and tried to calm her. "Shhh, there, there. There is nothing any of us could have done." She hugged her, and the other ladies gathered around. "Thank you all for getting a home ready for us." Then she shrugged and she admitted "Quite frankly, I never even gave a thought as to where we were going to live now, let alone sleep tonight." She smiled and looked at each one of them in turn. "Thank you all so very much. Each of you is a godsend."

The cabins of the cattle hands were all built down in the valley that lay about a mile beyond the grove. All of the residents who were home at the time of the attack were unaware of the devastation going on at the main house just a short distance away. The wives were preparing the evening meals and settling children in for the night. One of the ladies had caught a glimpse of an orange glow in the reflection of a mirror that hung on a wall in her cabin. She'd gone to the window and looked out to see the fiery hue above the silhouette of the trees against the darkened sky. Quickly, Lucy, another wife of a cattle hand, instructed her children to hide under the bunks and stay there until she came back. By the time she got outside, she met with other women who had also seen the sight, and together, they ran toward the grove. They stopped just beyond the trees, and there they stood frozen in awesome disbelief at the horrific sight.

Most of the men were in the foothills, in pastures miles away from anywhere as they tended the herds, repaired fences, and chased off an occasional predator. They knew nothing of what went on at the house or in the barns until late in the day, when their work relief rode out to them. In the late afternoons, they'd return to their homes to eat their evening meal and be with their families. The wives would catch them up on the goings- on while they sat and enjoyed the comfort of rocking chairs in front of a soothing, crackling fire. Tonight, though, they saw the strange orange glow on the northern horizon, and they knew trouble would be here to greet them. They hurried their horses along as fast as they could, gathered up lanterns, and rode to the yard of the house, ready to help with anything that needed to be done.

Martin awoke as Bubba, with another cattle hand's help, lifted him gently and carried him from the wagon into the cabin. Deliriously, he scanned his surroundings. Lamps lit the room, and he saw blurry figures of the people who stood all around him; their voices sounded muffled when they spoke. When he felt himself being lowered onto the soft mattress of a bed and then covered by a warm and comforting blanket, he felt safe and secure. Within minutes, he was fast asleep again.

Kathleen, Joshua, and Hattie thanked all the ladies and men for their help as they departed to settle into their homes for the night, each knowing that there would be much to do in the morning. Before they left, though, they reminded the siblings that they were close by, and if they needed anything of them, to please come and get them.

Their father settled, the family sat quietly and ate what they could of the food the ladies had brought for them. None of them had much of an appetite, but Hattie stressed the importance of keeping up their strength, for the sake of their father.

Joshua became restless. He took a bite then got up to look out the window for any signs of the sheriff or the doctor. "I should be out there helping them," he repeated each time he stood.

"They said for you to stay inside with us, Joshua," Kathleen reminded him in a gentle tone.

He ran his fingers through his hair, then as he sat again, he let out a loud, frustrated sigh. Just then, there was a quiet tap at the door, and he jumped up to open it. It was the sheriff. He removed his hat and stepped inside. Kathleen stepped closer to hear what he had to say.

"I just wanted to let you all know that Max is fine," he said. "He is home now, and he is asleep. We found Billy Joe. Doc's with him now, and he's gonna be alright too. He took quite a beating, though." Sheriff Taylor bowed his head and shook it sadly. After a moment, he placed his hat on his head and reached for the doorknob. "Oh," he added, as if he'd almost forgotten the rest of the message, "Doc wanted me to let you know that your daddy should sleep through the night. He gave him some strong medicine to help with that. And that Doc'll be sleeping in

Bubba's cabin, so if you need anything, go and get him. Otherwise, he'll be back first thing in the morning to check on you all." He and Joshua shook hands and Kathleen gave him a thankful hug. "Go and get some sleep now," he ordered. "All of you. You're exhausted." He stepped out and closed the door quietly behind him.

Suddenly, all the energy seemed to fall from Kathleen's body, and she felt the fatigue that the sheriff had referred to. Slowly, she dragged herself to her father's bedside and kissed his forehead. "I love you, Daddy," she whispered. Then she turned, and with Hattie's arm around her, they said their good nights to Joshua, walked into the adjoining room, and closed the door.

Joshua took his place in the rocking chair near the fireplace so he could be near his father. As soon as he sat down, sleep took him away quickly, and the entire family slept soundly through the night.

Chapter 6

The hoof beats of an approaching horse caused Alex to wake with a start. He swung around to find the horse with a female rider as they trotted near. Feeling groggy, he yawned and went to rub the sleep out of his eyes when he realized that he was completely naked except for the shirt that lay across his midsection. In a panic, he looked up again and saw that the rider was Kathleen. In that same moment, she saw him.

Awkwardly, he worked to arrange his shirt in attempt to cover himself a bit better. She pulled hard on the reins, and the horse came to a quick halt at Alex's feet. Her mouth dropped open, and her eyes widened with surprise. Even though she was embarrassed by the sight, she could not force herself to look away.

Embarrassed, he looked up at her, flashed a sheepish grin, and managed to squeak out an awkward greeting. "Hi."

"Mr. Johnson!" Kathleen blurted, her eyes still locked on his nakedness. "I... I... I didn't expect..." Finally, she was able to cover her eyes and turn away.

"Stay like that!" Alex ordered, then quickly stood and pulled his trousers on. After he donned his shirt and felt he was presentable, he was able to relax a bit. "Alright," he assured her. "I'm decent."

Slowly, she turned her head back to face him as she shyly peeked through her spread fingers. She found it was safe to look at him. This was the first time she had ever seen an undressed man, and to her surprise, she found the experience to be quite pleasant. She nervously looked at him, and when their eyes met, she shyly turned to look away again. She gazed out over the pond, and after she gained some composure, she asked him, with a jest in her tone, "Hotel too crowded, Mr. Johnson?"

Nervously, he fumbled to find words of explanation. The truthful version of the events that led him here would not make an appropriate story to tell the lady, so he tried to think of something else to say. "Uh, no," he stuttered. "It's just that… I…uh…" Then it came to him. "I couldn't sleep after all that had happened, so I came out here to be in the fresh, cool air." There was a slight pause before he added, "You know, to clear my lungs better." He faked a cough. He knew Kathleen would have to accept that story because she was a witness to how much smoke and soot he had breathed in the night before.

"Oh, yes." She smiled, then dismounted and added, "Well, I'm sure Daddy won't mind that you slept here." She felt more at ease with his presence, and as she continued to speak, she walked to the water's edge. "After all, you did save his life." She turned back to look at him. "We will always be grateful to you for that, Alex."

"Oh." Alex scratched his head. "I didn't realize this was your daddy's property." He looked around. "I guess I just rode until I saw this here pond and decided it was too beautiful a place to pass by."

She nodded her head. "I know what you mean." She knelt to pick up a pebble, then gave it a sideways toss and watched as it skipped across the water. "This is my favorite place in the whole world."

Alex sat and pulled on his boots. "I can see why," he replied as he admired the beauty that stood before him. She was the most exquisite creature he had ever laid eyes upon. He walked down to stand beside her at the water's edge, then turned to look at her. "Miss Sheldon," he began, "I am so very sorry about what happened to your family."

Kathleen turned to face him. "Thank you, Mr. Johnson." She tried to hold back her tears as she smiled back at him. In a playful tone, she added, "And stop being so formal. Please call me Kathleen." She held out her hand to him. "It's very nice to meet you, Alexander Johnson."

He took her hand in his and looked into her eyes. "The pleasure is all mine, I assure you." He smiled.

She gently pulled her hand from his, then gathered up her skirt and turned away. She looked at him over her shoulder as she held out her hand, then asked him, "Will you walk with me, Alex?"

A wave of excitement ran through his body at the chance of this opportunity. "Of course," he replied. He held out his elbow for her to take and added, "I would love to." Slowly, they began to walk along the water's edge.

As they strolled along, they talked and got better acquainted. They spoke of favorite things, childhood memories, Alex's origins, Kathleen's mother, and numerous other topics. Time slipped away, and so did thoughts of things outside of themselves. They were nearing a small cove on the other side of the lake when suddenly, the commotion started. The ducks had discovered their whereabouts, and Kathleen laughed joyfully as she dug in her pocket for the bag of crumbs. At first, Alex wasn't quite sure what to make of it all, but then he noticed the tens of ducks that came their way like a swarm of bees protecting their hive. "Do we run?" he laughed.

Kathleen grabbed his arm. "Don't you dare, for if you do, they shall surely attack." She played along. Gently, she took his hand and turned it over to pour some of the bag's contents into it. "Here, soldier. Use this ammunition to protect yourself," she playfully commanded.

Together, they played and laughed as they fed the ravenous fowl until Alex exclaimed, "I'm all out, Captain!" Then he grabbed her around the waist and effortlessly picked her up as he pretended he was going to throw her into the water. "You must go in and keep them busy. Sacrifice yourself and give the rest of us a chance to get away!"

Kathleen squealed with delight as she wiggled to free herself from his grip. She laughed so hard she could barely breathe, and her body went limp with exhaustion. He lowered her to the ground, then reluctantly released her when she was stable. She turned to look at him. Still breathless, she giggled until her eyes met with his. Their smiles faded, and they became hypnotized in each other's gazes. She smiled, breaking the trance, then turned her gaze to the satisfied ducks as they swam away.

A thought came to him and he took out his pocket watch. "I should accompany you home, Kathleen. I'm not really sure what is expected of me at the store today, but I've got to go find your brother and see what I can do."

"Joshua is still at the cabin with Daddy," she told him. "Let's go and you can speak to him there." As they turned to walk back to their horses, she added, with a bit of hope in her voice, "Maybe Daddy will be awake!"

They followed the fence line to a gate. Alex opened it and led Banjo through; side by side, they rode to the cabin.

Martin woke up for the first time that morning as soon as Doctor Holbrook tapped on the door at six o'clock. "You're just in time, Doc," Joshua said as he opened the door. "He's just waking up, and the morphine has worn off."

Doc saw Martin's grimace and went to his side directly. "There, there, Martin," he said as he filled a teaspoon with the drug. "Take this."

Reluctantly, Martin did as he was told, then lay back on the pillow to wait for it's effects. "I don't want to get hooked on that stuff, Doc."

"You won't, Martin, if you take it like I tell ya to." He put the bottle back in the bag. "Now then, let's take a look at those wounds." He got up to move back the covers so that he could work on Martin's legs. When he was finished, he gave Hattie and Joshua instructions so that they could tend the burns and change the bandages as needed, when he himself wasn't around to do it.

When the doctor was finished, Hattie offered the three men some coffee, then took some broth to Martin. "Would you like to try to eat something, Mr. Sheldon?" She sat at the side of the bed and offered him the liquid. He slurped it up readily while Doc and Joshua sat at the table and talked almost in whispers.

"What are you guys talking about?" Martin demanded. "I want to know what's going on." He tried to raise himself up to join them, but when the burning pain stabbed him, he relaxed again.

Joshua answered, "He's telling me about Max and the other men, Daddy."

"What about them?" Again, Martin's tone was demanding.

"Max is fine, Pops. He's at home, in his bed, resting," he replied, then went on to tell him about his injuries and the other men's, and finally about the loss of the brothers Ross and Robbie.

Martin's expression went from relief for Max to sorrow for the boys. "How about the rest of the men?" he asked. "And the barns and stables? And how about everyone's homes?" His voice had a note of panic.

Doctor Holbrook stood, walked to him, and laid a comforting hand on his shoulder as Joshua continued to speak. "All the other men are accounted for." He went into detail about how they were working on the range with the herds and didn't know about any of the goings-on at the house until it was too late. "And all the other buildings on the ranch were unharmed." He hung his head as he continued. "The Arabians are gone."

"But," the doctor chimed in, "Zack Thomas and some men are out this morning, looking for them. If the Indians didn't take 'em, the men will bring them back."

"Indians?" Martin jerked with a start. "What Indians?" The other two men looked at each other and realized that Martin was unconscious through most of what had happened, so this was the first time he had heard the truth. "They've all moved from this area, so it can't be true." Martin gently pushed Hattie's hand away and thanked her. "I can't eat any more."

"I saw them myself," Hattie told him as she set the bowl down and wiped the corners of his mouth.

Doc stood up and gathered his stuff. "It's true, Martin." He continued to tell about other places that had been vandalized or things that were stolen. "Up until now, everyone just thought it was harmless bandits or kids and their pranks, because no one was hurt. But now we know better, and we also know that these things are all related."

Just then there was a knock at the door. It was Bubba, and he was sad to report, "We only found a few of the Arabians." He looked down. "We couldn't find Prince, sir, but Monarch and the foal are safely back in the stable."

"Little Blaze was likely to slow them up, I guess," Joshua concluded.

The men continued to talk of the problem at hand, and Doc explained to them that the word in the territory was that this was happening all around because of the expansion of the railroad and the new settlements that were being built. "We're moving in on their territory, and they don't like it."

As the men sat and pondered the doctor's words, Kathleen entered the cabin with Alex just behind her. They all looked up, and Martin recognized Alex immediately. Kathleen ran to his side. "Good morning, Daddy." She smiled and pulled up a chair beside him. "How are you feeling?"

Martin assured her he was fine, but his eyes couldn't leave Alex. "You." He pointed at him. "You came into the house." Alex walked to the bed and took Martin's offered hand. "Thank you, son. I'm indebted to you."

"That's not necessary, sir," Alex replied. "I'm just thankful that I was able to help."

The other men in the room silently and unanimously agreed that the conversation was over for now, and they dispersed. The doctor bid the family a good day, and left to go to his next appointment. Bubba returned to his duties outside. Then Joshua spoke. "Daddy, I'm thankful that you're alright, but Alex and I have to get into town. We've got a business to run, right?" He looked at Alex.

"Right," Alex replied. "I'm glad you're alright, too, sir." He tipped his hat to the ladies, and the two men walked toward the door.

Kathleen hated to see him go. When she walked after them to the door, she paused to watch them leave. She hopelessly rested her head on the door frame and sighed as she silently bid Alex a fond farewell. Slowly and reluctantly, she closed the door, and when she turned around, she found Hattie's eyes on her suspiciously. "What?" she asked innocently. Not waiting for an answer, she began to clear the table to clean the breakfast dishes.

Hattie smiled knowingly but said nothing, for she had always known this day would come.

Chapter 7

Alex had just finished his delivery rounds as he stopped the wagon near the store room dock of the mercantile. Joshua had just locked up for the night when Alex called to him. "Hey, I'm glad I caught you." He unlatched the harness from the horses and started to lead them toward the stable. "I was hoping you'd join me for dinner and maybe a few beers afterwards."

Joshua smiled at him. "I'd be a fool to turn down an offer like that! You get them horses put away and I'll finish locking up. Meet ya out front."

As the two men walked toward the restaurant, Alex dug into his pocket to get the money he had collected on the route. "Keep it," Joshua instructed. "It's payday."

"But Joshua," Alex explained, "it's almost thirty dollars."

"That's great then." Joshua smiled at his friend. "That means we had a good week and that most everyone paid for their goods instead of charging!" As they continued to walk, he explained to his dumbfounded companion. "Look, I don't have the time to do it myself anymore, and my store is the only one within fifty-some miles that sells some of the most needed supplies. As long as people pay their bills, I make enough profit to let you keep three days' worth of delivery money." He continued to talk as they walked along the dusty main street of town, gesturing as he spoke. "Look, before you came along, I worked, I ate, and I slept, then I worked, I ate, and I slept. Now," he winked at Alex, "I work, eat, play, *then* sleep, if ya catch my meaning." He gave him a playful jab in the arm with his elbow and let out a mischievous chuckle.

Alex knew he referred to the time he'd spent with a certain young lady. He'd seen them together a couple of times, but Joshua never spoke about her. Alex respected his privacy and didn't ask any questions. He just thanked him with a nod and a smile, then returned the money to his pocket as they continued to walk.

The fire had destroyed nearly everything, and the things that were not burnt to ashes, were camouflaged among the charred debris. After Hattie had found and salvaged a small metal box containing some of her most precious possessions, including a photograph of her husband and his wedding ring, Kathleen decided to see what she could uncover. She was amazed to find some trophies that her father had won showing Prince at fairs, pieces of jewelry, and even some of her china dolls, unbroken. She looked them over and decided that they could be cleaned up, and she and Hattie could sew some new dresses for them. When she returned to the cabin, she was happy to show Hattie and her father what she had found. Although they were happy to see the items, none of them could compare in precious value to the treasures Hattie had uncovered.

Kathleen remembered Wilber only as well as she remembered her mother. He died just months before Anna. She remembered that it had been a very long and hot summer that year, and on that particular day, Martin had made it clear that no one was to work in the fields. But Wilber, being a strong man and a devoted worker, knew how important it was to get the hay cut so it would dry by the end of the week, to ensure enough feed for the cattle for the upcoming winter. He was determined to finish the last five acres, even if he had to do it himself. Even if he had to die from the heat.

After supper was done, Martin was settled with the newspaper, Hattie and Kathleen had cleaned up the dolls, and had begun to cut out patterns for their new dresses when there was a knock at the door. Kathleen got up to answer the summons, but before she got to the door, Joshua opened it and came inside, followed by Alex. They each carried a crate filled with goods from the store. "Good evening, everyone," Joshua greeted them.

Kathleen and Alex discreetly exchanged smiles.

Martin sat up slowly and asked, "What's all this, son?"

"Food and clothing for my wonderful family," he replied as they set the crates down, then went back out to the wagon to get more. Kathleen watched the doorway after them and anticipated Alex's return.

"Joshua," Martin cried. "What are you doing? Where is it all coming from?"

Kathleen and Hattie smiled as they happily began to go through all the boxes. There were new dresses and shoes, and Hattie blushed when she pulled out the new undergarments.

"I hope you're keeping track of all of this, son, 'cause Kathleen will withdraw the money tomorrow and pay you for it."

"Aww, shucks!" He looked at Alex. "Did you write all this down?"

Alex played along. "No." He shrugged. "I thought you did." He flashed another smile at Kathleen as she sat and enjoyed the little game they played. She found it difficult to take her eyes off him.

Joshua shrugged as well, and then the two of them headed back out to get the last of the crates. "You don't make any money that way, son. Didn't I teach you anything?" Martin asked, then called to Hattie, "Get a pencil and write all this stuff down."

"Hattie, don't you dare." Joshua pointed his finger at her and playfully warned. "Besides, Daddy, most of this stuff is donated by the people of Augusta. You *have* to accept it because they are all friends of yours."

Martin was defeated, yet he felt humbled to have such wonderful friends and family. "Well, in that case, please thank them for me and tell them if there is anything I can do for them to just let me know." Martin was a kind person, and he always tried to help people when they were in need. The people of the town were happy that they got a chance to give back and that this time Martin couldn't object.

"I love you, Pa," Joshua said, then turned to the women. "Now, you ladies keep on taking good care of him, and if you need anything, just ask either of us." He gave Hattie and Kathleen each a rib-crushing hug, and after Alex shook Martin's hand and wished him well, they turned and walked toward the door. Once again, Kathleen followed him to the door to watch him leave. Once he was in the wagon, Alex tipped his hat to her, and she smiled. It wasn't until after Joshua swatted the horses and they began to move that she closed the door. This time, Martin noticed, and he and Hattie exchanged smiles, but neither said a word as Kathleen hummed as she continued to put away the goods. She wouldn't have heard them anyway.

Later that night, Kathleen lay awake in her bed and thought about the fervent smiles that Alex secretly sent her way. She hugged her pillow tight, then closed her eyes and quickly, drifted off to sleep.

Alex, too, thought about those smiles as he lay in bed, but he didn't find sleep as easily. This was becoming the norm for him. Although he had just met Kathleen a few days ago, he felt like his life was complete now. He no longer had the desire to travel and see the frontier. He no longer had the desire to work on the railroad or ride in the Cavalry. He finally felt like he was home. He decided that he would write another letter to Aunt Rose and Uncle Marcus and tell them he was going to stay here. It would make them very happy to know that he was safe, settled in one place, and in love.

Chapter 8

"Daddy!" Kathleen shrieked when she and Hattie entered the cabin. "What are you doing out of bed?" she demanded. They set down the buckets of water they carried and quickly went to his side. Each took an arm and led him back to the bed.

Startled, Martin allowed their assistance, and once he sat on the edge, he replied, "It's been four weeks since the fire and I'm tired of being bedridden." He looked up at Kathleen with a smile, then added, "At least it didn't hurt so badly this time." He had a hopeful expression on his face.

"You mean to say this isn't the first time you've pulled this little stunt?" Kathleen gasped as she propped her hands on her hips. "Daddy, I am shocked at you!"

Martin raised his hands to calm her, then made her a promise. "I'll be good, if you'll ride into town and see if Doc Holbrook can come out and pay me a visit today. I've just got to get out of this cabin and do something," he reasoned. "I'd like to start rebuilding our home soon, and I can't start any planning, or anything else for that matter, from this bed." He emphasized his sentiment by smacking his hands down on the mattress, partially because of feelings of defeat, but also in the hope that his display of discouragement would get her to agree.

She let out a sigh. "Alright. I will go and see him." Then, as she shook her finger at him, she added, "Under one condition. You have to promise me that you'll stay right here until I get back."

Martin ran his finger across his chest to form an *X*. "I promise." He smiled. "Cross my heart."

Later that day, while the doctor was in the cabin with her father, Kathleen went outside to see to her horse and the foal. She was brushing Monarch when Max, who was completely recovered and back to work as usual, came out of the stables and gently took the brush from her hand. "Looks like you've got company." He pointed at the rider who approached on horseback. She raised her hand to shield her eyes from the sun and gazed out to the lane where she saw Alex drawing near. Once he got to the barnyard and dismounted, she walked to him and said hello.

"Hello, Kathleen," he greeted her as he removed his hat. "How are you this afternoon?"

"I'm fine, Alex, thank you," she replied. "To what do we owe the honor of your visit?"

He gave a friendly wave to Max, then replied, "Well…" He began to fidget with his hat. "I'm here to see you, Kathleen. Would it be alright if we took a little walk?"

"Of course." She looked at him curiously, then she turned to Max, who was shooing her away with a hand gesture. She turned back to Alex with a smile, and she took his arm as they began to walk. They usually headed in the direction of the pond, which had become Alex's favorite spot on the ranch as well. Their frequent walks often began in silence, but today Kathleen felt like Alex had something to say. She remained silent and allowed him the time he needed to begin the conversation. As they walked along, he occasionally glanced down at her and smiled. She smiled back. When they reached a wooden bridge that crossed over the playful stream in their path, Alex stopped and put his elbows on the rails. As he looked over the edge at the clear water beneath them, he seemed to become lost in deep thought. Kathleen couldn't help but wonder why he seemed troubled. She went to him and placed her hand on his arm. "Alex, is something wrong?"

"No, Kathleen, there is nothing wrong," he replied as he turned to face her. "I'm just trying to figure out how to tell you something." He took a deep breath and exhaled, then took her hands into his and gazed deeply into her eyes. "Kathleen, ever since I met you, my whole life has changed." He stopped and took in another breath to calm his nerves so he could continue. "I can't get you out of my mind. When I go to work, I look at your brother, and I see you." He laughed for a moment, then added, "And no, it's not because you two look alike." He smiled, then continued. "When I'm out on deliveries, I'm always looking for you to ride past me. When I go to sleep, you invade my dreams." He gulped hard, then said what he wanted to say. "I've fallen in love with you, Kathleen. Ever since the first day I laid eyes on you, I couldn't imagine my future without you in it. I want to spend the rest of my life with you. That is"—he paused—"if you want to be with me."

She stood motionless as he held her hands in his. His anxious demeanor had caused her to feel a bit apprehensive, as if he was going to tell her that he had to leave Augusta and go back home to his family. She wasn't prepared for him to say the words she heard, and it left her speechless. As she looked into his eyes and thought about his confession. She realized that he could have taken those same sentiments directly from her thoughts. He, too, trespassed into her thoughts, even at the most intimate of times. She felt her face grow warm. *Is this really what love feels like?* she wondered. *Does it mean you love him when he's always in your mind, and when you finally see him, your knees grow weak, your heart melts, and you stutter your words when you try to speak? And is it love when you watch him ride away and you feel like he's taking a part of you with him? And then you worry that something may happen and you may never see him again?*

Gentlemen had come to call in the past, but none of them had ever confessed such feelings, nor created them inside of her. Dumbfounded, she had no idea about what to say or even how to react.

"Kathleen, can you please say something?" Alex plead nervously.

"I feel the same way, Alex," she replied when he brought her from her deep thoughts. "I mean, just now as you spoke, it seemed as if you were describing exactly how I feel about you."

His shoulders relaxed and his smile grew as heard her words. He took her into a tight embrace and swung her around as they laughed together. Then, gently, he set her down. His smile slowly began to fade, and his expression grew serious as he continued to gaze into her eyes. Time froze, and they stood motionless. He could have counted the flecks of gold in each of her irises. Her beauty caused him to lose control of his gentlemanly patience, and he took a half step closer to her. His fingertips traced the length of her arms from her shoulders to her elbows, then found their way to her waist before they slowly slid around to the small of her back. As he did so, her hands moved to his chest, but her eyes remained focused on his. He carefully and lovingly pulled her to him to mold her body to his. When his gaze moved from her eyes to her full, delicious lips, his warm breath grew shallow as he hungrily moistened his own lips with his tongue. "I want to kiss you, Kathleen," he told her. "I've been dying to kiss you for weeks now." He was nearly breathless as he swallowed hard to dislodge the lump that had formed in his throat. Before she could answer, he leaned to her and brushed his lips lightly against hers. She felt their softness along with the warmth of his breath, and she slowly closed her eyes.

After a few seconds, his lips came again—this time, they stayed.

Kathleen wasn't sure what to do, so she just stood there with her eyes closed and her body pressed against his. A moan escaped her throat, and when he pulled his lips away, she opened her eyes to find his gaze fixed on her once again. He raised his hand to trace his finger along her jawline. Then, gently, he cradled the back of her head as he moved in for another kiss. This time, there was a passion that Kathleen had never known, but she accepted it and felt its rapture. Gently, he parted her lips with his tongue, and as it entered into her succulence, their breaths quickened, and together, they discovered rapture. Another moan slipped from Kathleen, and when she pulled him closer, she felt her body grow warm. She began to shake with excitement from the unfamiliar pleasures.

Alex's kisses grew hungrier as her tongue met his and he was able to taste the sweetness that her luscious lips hid. His embrace grew stronger, and he pulled her closer as he tried to devour every drop of the savory nectar she produced. His lips molded more firmly to hers as his kisses grew even deeper and his desires grew even stronger. When another moan escaped her, he came to his senses and pulled away to look at her. Her eyes were still closed, and she was breathless as she awaited his lips' return. "Are you alright?" he asked with concern as he brushed a stray hair from her face.

She smiled as she slowly opened her eyes. "Yes, I'm alright." She laid her head on his chest and snuggled into his embrace. He stroked her hair as they stood there for a while longer, and when they both had cooled down and their breaths were back to normal, they agreed it would be best if they just continued their walk. So they did so, hand-in-hand, making small talk along the way. They followed the path near the lake, and since they had no treats for the ducks, they decided to turn around. It was getting late, the sky was beginning to darken, and a cool breeze began to blow.

When they arrived back at the house, Alex accompanied Kathleen to the cabin to pay his respects to Hattie and Martin. While he was inside, he asked Martin's permission to escort Kathleen to the Augusta annual festival, which would be held in just a few short weeks. Of course, her father said yes, and so the plans were set that they would all ride in to town together. Alex always had a smile on his face when he left the ranch and the company of the Sheldon family, but this night, his smile was much wider and more confident. His deep feelings for Kathleen were out in the open now, and he no longer had to wonder about her feelings for him. He mounted Banjo as though he had springs in his heels, and then gave him the signal to go. He began to whistle a happy tune as they made their way down the dusty trail toward town.

Chapter 9

The day of the festival had arrived. Dr. Holbrook had told Martin that as long as he used his cane and sat to rest when he needed to, he would allow him to go. Kathleen and Hattie had just finished sewing their new dancing dresses the night before, and now they were excited to wear them. On their way to town, Martin and Hattie rode quietly on the front seat of the wagon, and Kathleen and Alex rode in the back, their feet dangled over the open back gate. Normally, Martin and Max would go on ahead and get the livestock ready for judging, but because of the recent devastation at the ranch, they were just going for the festivities and to enjoy themselves. Martin couldn't remember a celebration where he wasn't involved in the competitions. This one would be new to him, and he was as excited as the rest of the family.

He and Hattie and he were involved in their own conversation while Alex and Kathleen secretly held hands as they entertained themselves. Alex would reach over to tickle her, and she would playfully push him to his own side of the wagon and quietly giggle as she demanded that he mind his manners.

Martin and the ladies were even more excited about going to the festival this year, because when Martin invited Joshua to accompany them, he politely declined and announced to the family that he already had an escort to the event. He told them that he was going to introduce them to a lady who had recently moved to Augusta, who he had recently begun to court. He wouldn't tell them any more than that, but the family was delighted to find out that he had met a nice young woman.

When they arrived, and just as Martin climbed down from the wagon, they all saw the couple as they emerged from the crowd of people gathered around the hog roasting pit. Joshua, who half-ran with excitement, had grabbed his lady friend's hand and nearly dragged her to where Martin had stopped the wagon. The young lady didn't seem to mind the rush at all—in fact, she seemed just as thrilled as he was. She giggled happily and held on to her bonnet with her free hand as they dodged around people to come greet them.

When Joshua introduced her as Angela Potter, Martin took her hand and told her with a smile, "We are all very delighted to meet you, Miss Potter."

Kathleen watched the couple, and she could tell that they were very fond of each of each other. She could see that Joshua was overjoyed with love; if by nothing else, the grin he wore as he watched her intently was evidence enough. Kathleen was very happy for her brother.

"Likewise," she replied through a pretty smile. She had the fairest skin Kathleen had ever seen, and her light blue eyes seemed to smile whenever her lips did. Her hair was long and blonde, with thick wavy curls that fell free from under her bonnet. Kathleen watched them together, and she could tell that they were in love. She was very happy for her brother. "I am so happy to meet you. Joshua has told me so much about all of you, and oh," her dainty fingertips went to her mouth, "I am so sorry to hear about your home and your injuries, Mr. Sheldon. I am happy to see that you're doing better."

"Thank you, Miss—"

"Oh, please," she stopped him. "Call me Angela. All of you, please, call me Angela." She smiled pleasantly as she looked at each of them individually.

"Alright, Angela, and you call me Martin." He smiled, then added, "And I thank you for your concern. We are all doing very well now."

They visited a short while longer before everyone agreed it was time to get something to eat. Kathleen and Alex lingered behind the rest of the group, and Alex playfully whispered of his desires to hold her and kiss her.

Kathleen giggled and suggested they sneak off and go to his room in the hotel. "No one would ever find us there and then you could kiss me all day...*and* all night." She smiled, not really knowing the gravity of her words or the effect they had on Alex.

He cleared his throat, then replied in a gruff whisper, "Don't tempt me!"

The festival was a huge success. It seemed everyone who lived in and around Augusta, including surrounding towns, was there. The first events were the livestock shows, which Martin wanted to attend in the hope that he might find inspiration to rebuild his horse herds. Later, there were games to play for the children and competitions for the adults.

Joshua and Alex took part in the arm wrestling tournament, with their ladies at their sides to cheer them along. Kathleen watched in awe as Alex rolled up his sleeve to play the game. The sight of the muscles bulging in his arm brought back memories of the morning she found him asleep and nude by the pond. She remembered how he looked as he pulled the shirt to cover his body and how she almost wished the garment hadn't been there at all. She remembered how his chest hair grew sparsely over his chest, down his abdomen and into the depths of the unknown hidden below the buttons of his trousers.

Her mind drifted to the day he kissed her, and as she watched him now, those same feelings of desire returned. She wanted him to kiss her again. She wanted to feel that warmth and that passion...

Suddenly, the cheers of the crowd hindered her train of thought, and she caught herself as she stared at him indiscreetly. Quickly, she glanced around to see if anybody had noticed, and thankfully, no one had. All the excited focus was on the match. In the end, Alex had won all but the last round. Perry, the blacksmith, took home the trophy.

At twilight, a few of the townsmen got their band together for the traditional dance. This was the part that Kathleen had anticipated, for this was the only time that it would be proper for Alex to hold her in his arms in public. Everyone walked over to the steps of the mercantile, which was the only building in town that had a porch high enough to accommodate the perfect stage. The street out front was the dance floor, and it was framed with hay bales where people could sit.

When the first song started, Martin held his hand out to Kathleen and told Alex, "I'm sorry, son, but it has always been a tradition for my daughter and me to have the first dance together."

Alex stepped aside and replied, "But of course." He handed Kathleen's hand over to her father and added, "I would never stand in the way of a great tradition!" He smiled and allowed Martin to whisk her away to the dance floor.

After the second song, they returned, both laughing and panting. Kathleen sat on the hay bale beside Alex, and Martin, feeling he may have overdone it a bit, excused himself and went to find a more comfortable wooden chair. No sooner had Kathleen sat down than someone called out to her. "Kathleen!" the voice came, and she looked around. She recognized that voice as none other than her best friend, Timmy Swanson. Their families were neighbors when they were young, and they had often played together, until they were twelve and Timmy's father got a job in Newport and the family moved away. Now the only time they saw each other was at these yearly festivals.

"Kathleen," the voice came again, and then she saw him as he came toward her with his arms outstretched to greet her with a hug. He embraced her for a moment, then held her back. "Look at you! You are still as beautiful as always!" He looked around at her family with a smile, then asked them, "Isn't she the most beautiful creature you've ever laid eyes on?"

Embarrassed, Kathleen covered her face. "Stop it, Timmy."

Martin and Joshua acknowledged him with a familiar greeting, then Alex stepped forward and extended his hand. "Hello, Timmy," he said. "I'm Alex."

Timmy accepted the friendship gesture with a toothy grin. "Alex! Good to know you!"

"Oh, I'm sorry, Alex," Kathleen apologized. "This is my best friend, Timmy Swanson."

"Nice to know you, too," Alex replied with a smile and a nod.

As Timmy and Kathleen continued to visit and reminisce, Alex excused himself then left them alone and went to where Hattie sat and asked her for a dance. She accepted, and they disappeared into the crowded dance floor.

Timmy said his goodbye, hugged her one last time, and was about to walk away to rejoin his family when the musicians suddenly stopped playing and the banjo player fell to the ground. He had been struck in the chest by an arrow that killed him instantly. There were screams, and everyone began to run in all directions when they realized what had happened. Timmy grabbed Kathleen and told her to lie between the bales of hay.

Frantically, she began to call for Alex again and again, but Timmy kept pushing her down. She reluctantly did as he instructed, and after she was down, he covered her hiding spot with another bale of hay. She shook with fear as she lay curled up in the small space, her hands held tightly over her ears to try to block out the sounds of terror that filled the air.

Many natives ran out of the shadows of the buildings, and others jumped out of overhanging branches of the trees, while still more advanced on horseback. Their faces were painted, and they held arched bows loaded with arrows that they began to launch, one after another, into the crowd. They struck their targets accurately.

A few citizens of the town ran to retrieve their guns, and some shots were fired, but not enough. The attack was unexpected and far too sudden for anyone in the peaceful town to be prepared. Loud whoops and hollers from the natives began to drown out the screams and yells of the townspeople.

Alex pushed Hattie to the ground when an arrow stuck him in the leg, but the effort to protect her was useless when the same man followed his arrow with a knife in his hand. He stabbed her several times before Alex could get back up to his feet to stop him. As they struggled, Alex was able to pull an arrow from the brave's quiver and run it through the assailant's back, killing him. But it was too late. Hattie was dead.

Alex turned around just in time to see another brave as he came toward him. He reached up to catch the hand that held an ax aimed directly at his head. As they rolled on the ground, the native tried to free his hand, but Alex's grip was too strong. Alex managed to get him down to his knees and close enough to Hattie's body that he was able to grab the knife that had killed her. Alex swung it at his attacker and left a large, deep gash across his abdomen. The native stepped back as he looked down at the gash. He lost grip of his ax and fell to his knees as blood began to pour from the wound. He knew he was defeated. His eyes went to Alex as he stretched out his arms and let out a horrific yell. It was his death cry, and it was one of the most terrifying sounds Alex had ever heard. He saw pride in the man's eyes, which told Alex that he was ready to die for his people's cause, and Alex wanted badly to kill him. As he looked down at him, then over to Hattie's lifeless body, a fury that was unknown to him began to grow with his every exhausted pant. He raised his eyes and saw the devastation around him. He saw the bloody bodies of his newfound friends as they lay lifeless the street. This made his anger grow beyond recognition, and without further hesitation, he threw the knife hard and fast. It struck the brave deep in his chest and killed him.

When Alex stepped back and looked at what he had done, two more arrows flew at him and hit their marks. One pierced through his abdomen, and the other struck his shoulder and knocked him to his knees. The pain cut through his body with his slightest movements as he tried to look around to see where the arrows had come from. The next arrow lodged itself low in his back and forced him to lose all of his remaining strength. He fell to the ground helplessly, and then everything went black.

Suddenly, there was an eerie stillness in the air, and the only sound Kathleen heard was the crackling of embers that still burned in the hog pit. Paralyzed with fear, she shook uncontrollably as she struggled to crawl out of her hiding place and stand up. The sight was more gruesome than she could have ever envisioned. Bodies of familiar people lay bloodied everywhere. There was no discrimination and there was no mercy. The elderly lay dead, and so did the women and children. Some of the victims were even scalped. The ghastly sight made her vomit repeatedly, and it took a while for her to steady herself and regain her composure enough to stand and walk. Terrified, Kathleen scanned the area for a way to get to her family. Slowly, she began to walk as she shifted her eyes quickly from one slain and motionless mound to then next. She tried hard not to see the bloody reality before her as she prayed none of the bodies would be her family or Alex.

There's Timmy, Kathleen thought as she gazed mournfully into his empty eyes. She found it difficult to look away as she thought of how he had saved her life. *But what life is this*, she asked herself as she gazed around her blindly, *if everyone I know is dead?* Then panic struck as she frantically began again to search for her father and Joshua, for Hattie, and for Alex. Maybe they were alive. Maybe somebody else was alive. She had to look. *I can't be the only survivor, can I?* she asked herself as she nervously scanned the area. Kathleen tried to be hopeful as she looked for any slight movement or sign of life.

Suddenly, she heard a noise behind her, and slowly and cautiously, she turned around to see what had caused it.

It was a brown and white painted pony that stood just behind her and on his back, he carried a blood-stained native. As the young brave gazed at her, he held his hand over the wound on his temple. Blood streamed down his face, and though he looked a bit dazed, he continued to stare down at her, his eyes locked to hers.

Why doesn't he kill me? she wondered. Kathleen stared back at him with both fear and spite.

His face was painted with a red hand print that lay across his nose and mouth and his hair was long and black. What appeared to be the claw of an animal hung as an earring from his left ear, and teeth of another were made into a band that he wore around his upper arm. The lance that he held was decorated with feathers and a freshly cut scalp, which still dripped with the blood of its recently butchered owner.

She backed away slowly and he followed as he held out his hand for her to take. She shook her head and continued to back away from him. He guided his horse after her until she stopped. There were too many bodies around them, and she knew she would surely trip or fall, or worse yet, the horse would step on one if she were to continue. She knew the savage didn't care about that, but she did. Her only other option was to turn and run, but she dismissed that thought quickly. She could never outrun a horse. Once again, he held his hand out to her and softly grunted something that, to her, sounded like the word, "Come." As the sound came out, it must have echoed painfully in his head for his hand flew back to his temple and he cringed. After a few moments, he regained his composure, moved his horse closer, and once again, he held his hand out to Kathleen.

She looked around again, then concluded that there was no other place that she could go. Her eyes began to burn as tears formed. Her vision blurred and her body felt limp. She was defeated. Reluctantly, she turned her head away from him, closed her eyes as tightly as she could and surrendered. As soon as she held her hand out to him, he instantly, as if the opportunity would escape him, took hold. In one swift and graceful movement, he scooped her up and sat her in front of him, then he turned the steed and the three of them took off like a shot, toward the outskirts of town.

Chapter 10

They rode for miles into the late hours of the night by the light of the waxing moon. Kathleen drifted in and out of consciousness. She was barely aware of being jolted around by the horse's movements, and also almost oblivious to the arm that was wrapped around her as it held her on the paint. She was careless as to where they were going or what may happen to her upon their arrival. All she wanted to do was sleep and put this horrible nightmare behind her.

When the horse stopped, she awoke. They had come to a place where they would rest until sunrise. She looked around her and saw the silhouettes of the trees and sage brush, sand hills on the horizon, and the moon's reflection on a nearby stream. None of it looked familiar to her, but it didn't matter. Nothing mattered anymore. Life without her family. Without Alex. What was left to live for?

When the brave dismounted, he turned and reached his hand up to help her down, but she turned away from him. She slid down the opposite side of the horse and walked to the base of a tree, where she sat and stared into the darkness of the nearby woods.

The brave knew that she was in shock, and he felt sorry for her. Most native people felt hatred and anger toward the white men who had invaded their homeland, but he knew that the people killed tonight were innocent victims. He also knew that the fact that they were white made them the target for the attack. Many nations had declared war on all whites, women and children included.

⌒

Just as the sun peeked over the horizon, the native awoke to find Kathleen in the same place, still sitting at the base of the tree and looking into the forest. She didn't even move when he yawned and stood. He decided it would be alright to leave her for a short time, so he walked down the bank of a nearby creek to clean the blood off his head and to wash the rest of his body. When he returned, he led his horse to where she sat, mounted, then held his hand down to her. She stood slowly, and without looking at him, took hold. Just as easily as before, he scooped her up, and they rode on.

Kathleen did not see the fawn scamper off to its mother as they passed by. She didn't see the eagle as it soared overhead, nor did she register its cry as it called to its mate. All she could see were the bloody visions of the people she had left behind. She was still unconcerned about her fate upon arrival at their destination. Her life as she knew it was over anyway. *Why does anything matter anymore?* she thought as she gazed blindly into the distance. She didn't even care that the arm of a killer held her on the horse. She closed her eyes and grew limp, not caring if she fell and not caring if she lived.

⌒

Sometime later, she awoke to find that they had arrived at the village where the warrior lived. He was greeted by many other braves who seemed very happy to see him. Kathleen felt anxious as she looked around at the people who surrounded them. Villagers looked at her with mixed expressions, and some of them felt they needed to get close enough to touch her. She cringed and tried to pull herself away from their reach. Others looked excited, some seemed angry, and still others just came to briefly welcome the brave home, then turned and walked away.

As the horse made his way slowly and carefully through the people, an older lady came from the crowd, and the brave slid down and greeted her with a hug. Kathleen presumed this woman must be his mother, as she appeared to be very relieved to see him. She smiled as she cried while the other people cheered happily, and Kathleen concluded that, these people must have assumed him dead when he didn't return with the rest of their band of murderers.

With his arm around the woman, he led the horse, with Kathleen still mounted, to the front of an upside-down cone-shaped structure, which she assumed was his home. She looked around her and saw that there were many of these structures all around the village. She had heard about these tepees, but had never imagined she would ever see one up close. They were light tan in color, stood very tall, and each of them had colorful and unique designs painted on them.

Once they stopped, the brave held out his hand to her again, and once again, she refused it and slid down the other side. Some of the spectators chuckled and laughed, and the brave calmly laughed along as he gently took hold of Kathleen's arm and led her into the tepee. Here, he motioned for her to stay put. The joyous voices outside continued, but she put her hands to her ears as she tried hard to block them out. She walked to the side furthest away from the opening and sat down. Anxiously, she began to scan her surroundings.

Blankets were rolled up and stowed around the edges, a circle of rocks made a fire ring in the middle, and shields, weapons, and gourds hung on the rounded walls above and all around her. In a short time, the older woman entered, and Kathleen pulled her knees to her chest and wrapped her arms tightly around them.

The woman paid little attention to her as she sat in the middle of the tepee and began to make a fire. She had brought with her some articles that were unfamiliar to Kathleen, but as she worked with them, Kathleen was able to make out what they were. One was a tool used for cooking, and when the fire was hot, the woman began to cook. The smells from the food made Kathleen's stomach rumble, and she realized she was famished. She didn't want to take anything these people offered her, but as her hunger grew, she wondered if she would be able to refuse it.

While the food cooked, the woman motioned for Kathleen to come closer to where she sat on a rug. She was reluctant, but when the woman got up and walked to her, grabbed her arm, and pulled her with more strength than Kathleen could have imagined, she grew frightened and complied. The woman then motioned for her to remove her clothing, which Kathleen refused to do. Terrified, she turned and crawled back to the safety of her corner, curled up into a ball and began to cry. Once again, the woman got up, went to her, grabbed her by the arm, and pulled her back to the center of the lodge. She spoke words that Kathleen didn't understand, but her tone was harsh, so she did what she assumed she was being told to do. Slowly, she began to remove her clothing, and as she did so, she slammed her eyes closed tight and didn't open them again until after the woman had completely bathed her.

After the cleansing, a soft blanket was wrapped around her, and soon after, Kathleen heard a rustling sound of the makeshift door as it closed. She opened her eyes. The woman was gone. There by the fire lay a plate made from woven grasses, filled with a variety of steaming hot food. Beside that lay a dress. It was made from deer skins; the sleeves and skirt were fringed and the bodice was decorated with many tiny colorful beads, sewn in designs of intricate detail. Kathleen really wanted to eat and get dressed, but she was hesitant to wear a dress of these people. She looked for her own dress, but it was gone. Pitifully, she began to cry again and she forgot her hunger as she pulled the blanket tightly around herself and crawled back to the solitary corner.

When his mother came outside, the warrior was at the door to meet her. "How is she?" he asked with his gaze fixed on the door, in hopes that the lost girl would also emerge from the lodge.

Solemnly, she shook her head. "It will be a while, my son," she replied, then walked on. He stood a while longer and stared blankly forward as he regretfully wished they could have met under different circumstances. As it was, she was in shock, and he knew it would take her some time to work through her tears and sadness. He wanted desperately to help her, but as of now, he could think of nothing he could do, and it weighed heavily on his mind.

Chapter 11

A peddler waded his wagon slowly through the bodies that lay on the street of Augusta. He looked over the disaster and shook his head in awesome disbelief. By the evidence which lay before him, the traveler concluded that this massacre had just happened a day or two prior. Smoke rose from a still-smoldering building, and the air was just starting to fill with the smell of death. He decided the best thing to do first was to send a message of distress by telegraph to the closest town and notify them of what had happened so that they could send help. Graves needed to be dug and services held. Since he couldn't drive to the telegraph office because of the bodies that covered the street, he cautiously reached for his gun and climbed down from the wagon. He wasn't taking any chances, in case the assailants were still in town.

Once inside the office, he searched for clues of how to send a message. He came upon a code book with the different codes as well as instructions on how to run the telegraph machine. When he found the switch to turn the machine on, he tapped in the codes for the word "help" then waited anxiously for a reply. Within minutes, the machine came to life, but he did not know how to read it. He got up to leave the office, relying on his faith that the message was received and that the person who answered his plea would send help.

When he came out of the telegraph office, he scanned the area again, then called out to anyone who might hear. "Hello?" he shouted, and almost immediately, he heard the faint cry of a baby in the distance. Carefully, he dashed toward the sound, and within minutes, he recovered the young boy from under his mother's fallen body. His lips were parched from thirst, and his face was badly burned from the sun. The man took him back to the shade and protection of his rig and gave him some water and a few bites of a biscuit. He cleaned him up as best he could, and when the baby was settled, he began his search again. He touched each person as he walked by and felt for body heat or a pulse. When he found neither, he continued on to the next.

After about an hour, relief arrived from a nearby town in the form of a doctor, the sheriff, a minister, and ten of the town's concerned citizens. The peddler had recovered six living so far, and he had tended to each of them as best he knew how. He was exhausted and very thankful to see them all ride into the forsaken town. "Thank God, you're here!" He sighed with relief as he removed his hat and wiped his brow with his shirt sleeve. "I'm not sure how much more of this I can do." He backed away and sat on the steps of a nearby building, then placed his head in his hands and began to sob.

The sheriff walked to him and placed a calming hand on his shoulder. "This is too much for a hundred men to bear, let alone just you, sir. I thank you for all you've done." Then he turned his attention to the other men and ordered, "Let's get busy."

Several of the men grabbed shovels from the minister's wagon and made their way to the church yard to start to dig graves. Other men followed the minister into the center of the square to search through the fallen bodies while the doctor went, accompanied by another man, into the stable where the survivors were resting. The caring peddler had thoughtfully dragged them to the shelter to get them out of the elements and the heat of the midsummer sun. The sheriff went to the telegraph office to send a more accurate message of the massacre and the desperate need for more help.

By the end of the day, the Cavalry from a nearby encampment had arrived and helped with the burials. After funerals were performed, a unanimous decision was made. The town would be burned to the ground and all the survivors transported back to Pine Valley, the closest city, where they could be better cared for in the hospital.

Nearly two weeks went by before Kathleen was ready to come out of the tepee and see her new world. Shock and distress caused her to sleep most of that time, and since she hadn't eaten or drunk anything in that time, she grew very weak from dehydration and lack of nutrition.

The older woman had taken care of her the best that Kathleen would allow, and on this day, she was finally able to coax her into the dress and outside. The sunshine felt good on her skin, and as the fresh air filled her lungs, she almost felt energized. A tall form in front of her blocked nearly all the sunlight, and it took some time for her eyes to adjust. Soon she realized who it was. This was the first time she had seen her captor since their arrival to the village. His face wasn't painted now, and he stood tall and proud near the front of the door flap. Kathleen could see that he was a handsome man. As he looked down on her, she could see a gentle kindness in his eyes. She turned away quickly and refused to look at him. To her, he was a murdering savage, and she never wanted to see him again.

After a few moments, the brave turned and walked away. She let out a heavy sigh of relief and began to relax. The woman took her by the arm and led her. As they walked, Kathleen took in her surroundings. She found there were women and children everywhere. The women busied themselves with some sort of chore or tended to a need of a child. As she timidly walked along, she felt eyes upon her as some of them glanced up briefly from what they were doing. She noticed one young girl in the distance who looked to be around fifteen years of age. She seemed to glare at Kathleen in anger as they passed by and her apprehension grew, but her eyes continued to scan the area. There were children who sat on the ground and peacefully played games while others happily laughed and ran from still others that chased them. The smallest ones hid and shyly peered out from behind their mothers to peek at her in curiosity. She noticed a few elderly men who sat in a half-circle in front of the largest tepee in camp. In the distance, there were younger men on horseback, and closer in there was a herd of horses that roamed free. When she noted there were no fences to hold them, she couldn't help but wonder intently what kept them here.

Suddenly, Kathleen saw what she felt was a most beautiful sight. She gasped with joy as she saw a familiar woman draw near. She pulled her arm free of the older woman and ran to her. It was Dorothy Vickers from Augusta, and she, too, practically ran to greet her.

Kathleen began to cry with relief as they embraced. "Oh, thank God, I'm not the only one in this hell!" Kathleen exclaimed.

Dorothy hugged her tight, and as she stroked her hair, she comforted her but hushed her to silence. "There, there, now, child. You're safe," she said in a calming voice. "Everything is going to be alright now." She pulled away and held Kathleen's face in her hands as she gazed lovingly into her tear-filled eyes. "We're all going to be alright, dear. We've been saved." She smiled. Her eyes seemed to light up as the words flowed from her mouth.

Kathleen looked back at the woman and shook her head in disbelief. "Saved?" she asked. "How can you say that, Dorothy? These bloody sav—"

Dorothy silenced her. "Stop it, Kathleen!" she warned her. "Some of these people know English. You need to be very careful what you say." Her expression calmed again, and she continued with a carefree smile. "We should be thanking these people for saving us."

Before Kathleen could respond, the older woman had grabbed her by the arm again to take her back to the originally set destination. As she stared in disbelief, she allowed herself to be pulled along, and she watched Dorothy return to where she had come from. Kathleen decided that she must still be in shock or some kind of deep denial that neither of them could ever understand.

The woman led her to a group of other women who sat together and visited as they worked. Kathleen's eyes burned with tears that threatened to fall as she looked down at them. The older woman motioned to her to sit down with them. Timidly, she sat, and as she did, she looked around at each of them and at what they were doing. They held tools and used them to scrape across what looked to Kathleen to be animal hides pegged to the ground. The tools were used to remove excess skin and meat off the hides so they could be used for blankets and made into clothing and shoes. One of the women picked up an extra tool and handed it to Kathleen. Their eyes locked for a moment, then Kathleen turned away and fixed her focus on the tool. As she turned it over in her hands, she thought it appeared to have been made from the bone of an animal. *Or,* she thought grimly to herself, *another human that they butchered.* She dropped it immediately and brushed her hands off on her dress.

Once again, the woman picked it up and handed it to her, and this time, she let out a grunt as she did so. Kathleen looked into her eyes and she saw that she, too, seemed to have a gentleness about her. She took the tool and watched intently as the other women worked. This pleased the older woman, and she smiled and left Kathleen to learn with the younger woman.

After she watched the native women work a while longer, Kathleen's eyes began to wander. She saw Dorothy in the distance and she seemed to be very happy as she sat and worked among her circle of women. She appeared to be listening to them as she nodded and smiled while the other women talked. Then, just about the time she was about to shrug off the possibility that she was actually engaged in a conversation with them, all of the women in that group started to laugh at something that Dorothy had said. This angered Kathleen.

Right then, she decided to take detailed mental notes of her surroundings so that she could plan her escape. She knew she would have to go alone, and the thought of that frightened her, but it was apparent that Dorothy was at ease with these people. She knew she could never convince her to go with her or even to help her. She began to scan the area when her eyes suddenly stopped. In the distance, she saw another woman who appeared to be white. She also worked peacefully with the native women, and she appeared to be in conversation with them as though they were friends. Kathleen began to think that maybe she was going crazy. Maybe this was just a horrible dream that she couldn't wake up from. *Can this really be happening?*

Just then, the young lady beside Kathleen interrupted her thoughts when she took her hand in hers. She moved the tool around in Kathleen's hand to show her how to hold it, then she moved aside and motioned for her to try it. Kathleen obeyed. The other women smiled in approval and she continued to work. She decided that she would still plan an escape, though. There was nothing that could keep her here. She missed her father and Joshua, and she missed Max and Hattie. She missed the house, her room, and her bed. And she missed Alex. She wondered what he was doing right now. Were any of them looking for her?

Suddenly, as the thoughts of her family came to mind, tears formed in her eyes. Sadness and loneliness began to overwhelm her to the point that she no longer cared about the job she was doing. She began to cry uncontrollably, and then, as anger took over, and with all the strength that she could muster, she began to scrape the same spot, over and over, so much so that the tool nearly went all the way through the hide to the point that she could see the roots of the fur on the other side. The girl called out to try and stop her and when Kathleen didn't respond, she reached out and grabbed the sleeve of her dress and tried to stop her from ruining the hide.

Defensively, Kathleen swung around, took hold of both girl's wrists, and they began to struggle on the ground. The girl cried out in surprised horror as Kathleen rolled her over to her back, sat on her stomach, and pinned down her arms down. Within seconds, they were surrounded by onlookers, and the older woman stepped forward and seized Kathleen. With her hands over her mouth, Dorothy stood and watched in helpless distress as Kathleen kicked and screamed while the older woman dragged her through the dirt, and back to the seclusion of the lodge.

Chapter 12

Several weeks had passed, and all but one of the survivors of the massacre had been treated and released from the hospital. The resilient baby was healthy and strong, and a grateful childless couple in the town quickly adopted him. One of the survivors was Jacob Miller. Jacob had lived in Augusta with his family when he was young, but had moved to attend college in the East. There, he met and married his wife. They had come back for a few weeks so he could introduce her to his family and friends and to attend the annual festival. His wife and all of his family were found dead, and he didn't know any of the other survivors. Now he was alone.

Jacob had been released from the hospital two weeks prior, but he stayed close by for the man who still lay unconscious. Their beds had been next to each other in the ward, so Jacob felt a bit of a kinship with him. He spent most nights asleep in the chair across the room so he could be close to him when he awoke. This man, who slept virtually motionless for more than three weeks, was the one who was the most critically injured of them all. The rough and rugged travels to the hospital had caused healed-over wounds to reopen and bleed again. The loss of so much blood made the doctor feel hopeless and doubtful of his ability to heal, let alone survive through the first night. The surgeon cleaned and dressed the man's lacerations, and the staff did their best to make him comfortable. After they did all that they could, they left the rest up to the good Lord.

Jacob had been awake and coherent through most of his own hospital stay, so he knew all the procedures the medical staff had performed on the patient and all the moments that were touch and go. He saw all the struggles this man went through to stay alive, from the several times when his fever spiked to the time that he stopped breathing. A sound had happened to awaken Jacob that night, and when he got up to investigate, he noticed that the man wasn't breathing. He rushed out to get the nurse in charge, and together they shook him, called to him, and rolled him from side to side until eventually their efforts paid off and he took in a deep breath. Soon, his breathing returned to normal.

Many times, Jacob had spread a blanket over the man to warm a shiver, and many more times he had rushed over to comfort him when he let out a somber moan. Day after day, he sat with him, he read to him, he talked to him, and prayed for the day to come when he would awaken. He was all Jacob had, and this man was alone now, too. They would need each other to help heal their wounds.

Half awake, Jacob sat slouched in a chair, his feet propped on another, when two nurses came in to do their evening rounds. Through a slit in one eye, he saw one pick up the man's arm to check his pulse and the other pull the blanket back to check his wounds and the bandages. He closed his eye again just as one of the nurses spoke in a whisper, "Ethel, go and get Dr. Nelson." The other nurse replaced the blanket and quickly left the room. "There, there now, mister." She soothed him and gently held him down when he tried to move. "The doctor will be here soon. Shhh..." she said.

Immediately, Jacob sat up straight and strained his neck as he listened intently and tried to look around the heavyset nurse. He longed to rush to the man's side as he had so many times before, but then he paused and smiled as he heard the most wonderful sound he had heard in a long time. The man spoke.

"Wh...where, where am I?" he murmured faintly through dry lips. He tried again to sit up, but the nurse gently held him and he relaxed.

The nurse reached over to the bedside table, poured a small glass of water from the pitcher, and offered it to him. Gently, she placed her hand behind his head and helped him rise up enough to take a drink. "Just a sip now," she ordered in a whisper. "That's it. Nice and easy."

Soon the doctor, an exuberant and enthusiastic middle-aged man, entered the room with a huge, optimistic grin on his face. "Welcome back to life," he greeted as he picked up the chart and glanced over the notes in the documents. He began to scribble something down and added, "There was a time there when I thought you going to leave us." He handed the papers to the nurse, then came to the bedside and smiled. "I'm glad you decided to stay."

Through mere slits in his eyes, the frail man looked at the doctor and forced a slight smile until the weight of his open eyelids grew heavy and he had to close them again. He remained motionless as the doctor began to examine him.

The doctor listened to his heart, felt his forehead, and looked at his wounds one at a time, then gently and carefully touched several areas on the man's body. As he did so, he left lasting imprints of pain along the way, and the man cringed and moaned. The good doctor gently tried to comfort him. "There, there. I know that hurts, and I'm sorry to have to do that." Then he stopped, and his voice changed back to the energetic, cheerful tone. "You're healing very nicely, and you should be up and out of here in no time. But until then, you rest," he ordered, then covered him again with the blanket. "You know," he added, "you are very lucky that third arrow went into your pelvic bone and not just a teensy bit higher." His voice hit a high-pitched squeak, and as he spoke, he held up his thumb and forefinger to about half an inch's width to help demonstrate to the patient the difference between his life and his death. He wrote something more on the chart, and after he handed it back to one of the nurses, he asked, "Now then, sir, do you remember your name?"

The man slightly nodded, and after he strained to take a deep breath, he whispered on his exhale, "Alex." Then, as if saying the word took every ounce of energy he had left in him, he drifted back to sleep.

"Ha!" the doctor exclaimed in a loud boisterous whisper that startled the three onlookers. "Now, we can stop calling him 'Lucky Louie!' Write that on his chart," he instructed, and with a satisfied smile, he left the room.

The two nurses shook their heads and giggled quietly at the doctor's wit, then finished up their duties, said goodnight to Jacob, and left the room. When they were gone, Jacob pulled his chair to Alex's bedside, made himself comfortable, and then gazed at him intently, hopeful that his eyes would open again.

The next morning, Kathleen awoke to find two women entering the lodge. One was the older woman with whom she shared the home, and the other was Dorothy Vickers.

Protectively, she pulled the blankets up over her head and held them as tightly as she could as she waited for them to grab her and pull her out of the lodge. But then Dorothy began to speak to her.

"Kathleen, they want me to talk to you," she started. "They want you to know that you don't have to be frightened of them and that they do not intend to hurt you, or me, or any one of us." After some silence, she pleaded, "Please Kathleen. Talk to me."

Kathleen replied from under the covers, "Is that really what you believe?"

"Yes, Kathleen, I do. I know it's true." Her hand gently pulled the blanket down a little, and Kathleen looked into her eyes.

"Why did they bring us here, Mrs. Vickers?" she asked. "Do they want us to work for them as slaves?"

"No, dear," she replied. "They want to give us a home, to give us a new life and teach us their ways. They want to protect us and take care of us, and for us to work together, not *for* them, but *with* them, and to live here, with them, for as long as we wish to." She smiled.

Kathleen sat up and glared at Dorothy in anger. "Why would they think that we would want to live with them after what they did to our families and our town? Are they stupid? Don't they have enough of their own people to make a town? What makes them think they can steal other people and that we would be happy to live here, with them?"

Dorothy shook her head in confusion. She didn't know why Kathleen spoke this way about the people. "Kathleen," she pleaded with her, "these people *saved* us." She tried to explain, but the girl shook her head and refused to listen. Dorothy got up and pulled the blankets Kathleen was hiding under and tried again to talk to her. After a brief struggle, she managed to cup her face in her hands and gently forced Kathleen to look at her and hear her words. "For years my uncle has traded with these people, Kathleen. I've come to know them well. They are good people." When she found she wasn't getting through to her, she changed her tone. "Kathleen, these are not the people who attacked Augusta and killed our families." Kathleen's eyes opened and tears began to form. Dorothy continued in her normal, soft voice as she crawled up beside her and took her into her arms. "They came afterwards, my dear, and found all of us that the other ones missed." She gently stroked her hair as she continued. "*Us*, Kathleen. They saved *us*." She smiled as she held her and began to rock.

Kathleen pulled away to look at her, her face streaked with tears. "How can you say that, Dorothy?" she sneered at her. "I saw what happened!" she yelled.

"I saw what happened, too, dear," she replied in a calm voice. A tear ran down her cheek, then she sniffed and wiped it away. "Those other ones killed my Mary. If it was these people who killed her, do you think I would be so happy to be here?" she asked. Just then, a man's voice called to them from outside. The older woman answered, and the door flap opened. In walked Kathleen's captor. She shuddered and crawled under the covers and curled herself up as tightly as she could.

Dorothy spoke again. "This is Thunder Horse, Kathleen. Look here," she demanded as she pointed to his head where a scar had begun to form. Kathleen peeked out. "He was attacked, too." She paused. "When he was protecting you."

Kathleen slowly sat up as her thoughts began to spin, and she tried to piece the events together in her mind as she remembered them. She recalled the noises, the yells and screams of the confused people running all around her, and she remembered how Timmy hid her in the hay. She thought about how she had covered her ears with her hands to try to block out the sounds, and then suddenly, she remembered how odd it was that the noises had come to an abrupt silence. Her memory went back to when she stood and found this native behind her. Then it dawned on her. How did all of the other people go away so suddenly? *I must have blocked it all out! Is what Dorothy said really true?* Kathleen caught herself as she stared at the man and found that she couldn't take her eyes off of him. She took notice of the gentle kindness that she thought she had seen before. She was afraid to believe it was possible, but now she wasn't sure what to believe because Dorothy's words were starting to make sense. She actually knew these people, and they had saved them. "But how?" were the only words that Kathleen could think to say.

Slowly, so as not to startle her, the brave lowered himself to kneel on the mat in the center of the lodge, and then he spoke. "I will tell you, if you will hear what I say."

The sound of his voice as he spoke English left Kathleen speechless. All she could do was nod her head as her eyes grew wide with surprise.

Thunder Horse spoke the best he could, to explain to Kathleen how his hunting party came across the other tribe's war party. "My mother spoke of darkness coming. She did not know when it would come. And we have all heard the talks of attack on the white village, but we did not know who would make the war. My party was hunting one day when we saw warriors from another village. They were dressed for war. I went to our father and told him what we saw. He said it would be wise to follow, to see where they go.

"My men followed the warriors at a far distance for three days, and then we knew they go to the village of our friends. Our people and your people have been friends in trade for many years, and so we want to help. But we could not. We were too late. When we arrived, most of your people were already slain. Four women and some children lived, and so we brought them here, to stay with us. When I found you, you stood alone among the dead. Through the smoke, I saw an enemy warrior walk to you, his tomahawk ready, in his hand. I called to you, but you did not hear me. I fought with the man, and my knife found his heart, but not before his tomahawk found my head." He pointed to the mark on his temple. "When I got on my horse, I could not see well and I had much pain, but I looked until I found you." He paused and then asked, "Do you remember now?"

Kathleen shook her head. "I remember seeing people on the ground all around me, and then I remember seeing you behind me." Tears welled up in her eyes again as she dreadfully asked him, "You only saved women and children? Does that mean my father and my brother are dead?"

"All of the people they did not kill are here. They are women and children," he said, and he bowed his head in regret. "I am sorry." With that, he got up and walked to the door. He paused before he went out as he searched for something more he could say. There was nothing that would ease the girl's pain, so he left her to think on his words. The older woman got up and followed him out.

When they were gone, Kathleen weakly pulled herself back into her nest of robes, covered herself again, and wept. Never before had she felt so alone.

Dorothy stayed with her until she cried herself to sleep, all the while praying that the words Kathleen heard would give her some peace and help her to heal.

Chapter 13

Jacob fell asleep in the chair and didn't awaken again until late into the night when Alex called out in his sleep. He jumped up and was at his side in an instant and calmed him with a quiet voice. "Shhhhh." He touched Alex's shoulder gently, then reached for the half-full glass of water that still sat on the table. He smiled as Alex opened his eyes to look at him. "Are you thirsty?" he whispered.

Alex smiled slightly, then raised his head a little to accept the drink he offered. Once he lay back down, he whispered, "Are you the doctor?"

Jacob let out a loud chuckle, then quickly hushed himself. "Heck no, I ain't no doctor," he whispered. He held out his hand to Alex. "The name's Jacob Miller, and I want to tell you, it is my honor to meet you, sir."

Alex smiled again, then as he carefully raised his hand to take Jacob's, he replied, "It's a pleasure, Jacob." His voice was a strained, hoarse whisper. "I'm Alexander Johnson. It's good to know you." Then he shifted a little in his bed. "Are there any nurses here?" he asked sheepishly. "I need to relieve myself."

Jacob jumped up promptly. "Yeah, there is! I'll go and get someone." He began to leave the room, but instantly, a nurse with a bedpan appeared in the doorway. Jacob excused himself and left the room to let the nurse carry on with her duties and tend to the patient.

A little while later, after she had bathed Alex and cleaned up his bed, the nurse left, and Jacob peeked his head in from around the corner. Alex, who was propped up into a sitting position now, waved him in. "Wow, it feels good to be clean!" He looked at Jacob a bit sheepishly. "Sorry I was so offensive."

Jacob brushed it off. "Don't worry about it. I've smelled a lot worse things."

Alex looked at Jacob with a puzzled expression. Jacob instantly picked up on his confusion and began to explain. "I'm from Augusta and, well…" He paused. "I was there." His smile faded, and as he spoke, his eyes fell to his hands in his lap. "There were only six of us, Alex. You were hurt the worst." He reached up and unbuttoned the top few buttons of his shirt to expose a healed wound on his left shoulder. As he pointed to it, he explained, "The doctor said that if it had gone in an inch lower, I'd have been dead, too."

Alex sat up a bit and felt somewhat hopeful as he swallowed hard, then asked, "Where are the other survivors?" He almost dreaded the question.

Jacob's gaze stayed focused downward as he began to reply.

"I'm sorry, Alex. They were all brought in here to see you. The doctor thought it could be a way to identify you." He sniffed, then looked up at him and said, "None of them could tell us who you were."

Alex's gaze went blank as he pictured Kathleen's face in his mind. His expression grew peaceful, though, as he thanked God that the last time he saw her, she was smiling, happy, and alive and well. He doubted he could go through life with visions of her slain in the street. He reached out a hand to Jacob to reassure him that he was okay. "Thank you, my friend. Thank you for staying with me."

It wasn't until after hours of contemplation that Kathleen decided that what Thunder Horse and Dorothy had told her was the truth. Her absence of memory could not allow her to conclude otherwise. After she washed in some water that the older woman had left for her, she donned a clean dress and timidly went outside to join the people of her new community. She was immediately spotted by the older woman, whom Dorothy had told her was called Whispers To The Wind. She was a healer of the people, and sometimes, she was able to see things before they happened. Like the attack on the town, which was the darkness that Thunder Horse spoke of. She was also the very proud mother of the brave warrior called Thunder Horse. She had been very kind to her, Kathleen realized, even when her behavior was at its most impossible.

Kathleen timidly smiled in apology when she saw her, and Whispers To The Wind returned a smile, filled with forgiveness and reassurance. She held out her hand to Kathleen and coaxed her to follow. Kathleen did, and as they walked together, she noticed there were very few people in the village. They followed a little path that led into a grove of trees, and as they ducked branches and stepped over stones, Kathleen could hear the faint sounds of laughter grow louder and closer. When they came out on the other side of the woods, they were in a clearing where a stream ran through the grove and divided it. It was one of the prettiest places Kathleen had ever seen. The leaves on the tall cottonwoods reached endlessly upward, and their leaves appeared a silvery green color.

Tiny fluffs of cotton fell from them like snow from the skies, and they fluttered in the breeze until they came to rest on the ground. The stream looked playful and inviting as it dodged boulders and fallen branches on its way to the unknown. In some places, it seemed to be in a hurry as it trickled along, and in others, it formed small lazy pools where it seemed to take a break from its never-ending journey.

The mid-afternoon sun streamed in through the trees around the glen, in rays that looked like golden curtains blowing in the gentle breeze. Kathleen closed her eyes and raised her face up to feel the warmth of the glow. She felt like she could have stayed here, like this, forever.

Most of the other women were here, they talked and laughed, and some of them played as they caught the fish they would later clean to eat.

Kathleen timidly looked around at the ladies as they had fun, until her eyes settled on the young girl she had struggled with on her first day out of the tepee. The girl looked back, gave her a forgiving smile, and gestured a friendly wave. Kathleen smiled and waved back. Further downstream, there were other women who washed clothes and laid them out on large rocks to dry in the midday sunshine. When they were finished with that chore, they would come up to where the others were and join in the fun. Directly in front of her stood the girl who glared at her the day Kathleen came to the village. This time, Kathleen didn't look away. Instead, she smiled at the girl in a gesture of friendship. The girl turned and ran away as another person drew near.

Kathleen smiled, and tears of relief formed in her eyes as she saw Dorothy walk out of the stream and come towards her. Her arms were outstretched, and she held her close for comfort as she wept. "There, there, now, child." She stroked her tangled hair. "Everything is alright now, and we are safe." She withdrew and held her at arm's length, and Kathleen wiped her eyes and smiled a shaky smile.

"I know, Mrs. Vickers." Kathleen sniffed. "I'm so very sorry for my behavior."

"Ah!" Dorothy brushed her apology away into the wind. "I understand. And the people understand. And now, everything is going to be alright." She smiled as she stood straight and put her hands on her hips. "Now then. It's time you learned the ways of the people, for we will stay here at least until spring, and we have to pull our weight." She pulled Kathleen along as she began to walk back into the water, and she continued to talk. "Fall is coming soon, and it is too far and much too dangerous to be traveling anywhere now. If we want to return to a town and our way of life, some of the braves have offered to take us in the spring, when travel is safe."

"Fall is coming?" Kathleen looked at her in surprise.

"My dear." She nodded in reply. "It's late September now. Can't you feel it in the breeze?" she asked as she looked to the sky, stretched out her arms, and took in a deep breath through her nose.

No longer oblivious to her surroundings, Kathleen began to feel the slight chill she spoke of, and as Dorothy continued to talk, they stopped in the middle of the stream. "The snows will come soon, and the natives are planning to move the village into the hills, where we will all be safer from the winter storms. Look!" she exclaimed as a large trout came right toward where she stood. In a quick swoop, the tall thin woman leaned forward, swooshed her hands through the water, scooped upward, and sent the fish flying through the air and onto the bank into a pile with the other fish. She stood proudly with her hands on her hips again and said with a satisfied smile, "You try!" Dorothy backed away and gave her room.

Kathleen smiled shyly and looked around to find that all eyes were upon her. The women laughed and mimicked Dorothy's words as some of the younger ones clapped and chanted, "You try! You try!" Nervously, Kathleen took a deep breath and gazed down into the water.

"Alright now," Dorothy coached in a voice not much louder than a whisper. "Be still so that one will come. Too much commotion and they'll stay away." All the women quieted and watched intently.

Kathleen stood very still and watched the shallow water as it swirled among the various- sized rocks in its bed. She saw some minnows as they played hide-and-seek around a moss-covered stick, and a turtle that climbed out of the water to sun itself on the bank in the distance, but she could see no trout.

Suddenly, she heard, from behind her, "Shhhh." Then in a dramatic whisper, Dorothy added, "There's one right there." Her arm, with an extended finger, came over Kathleen's shoulder. About twenty feet away, she saw what looked to be a shadow that came from behind the cover of two big mossy rocks. It seemed to contemplate its escape route as it sat there idle, hovering patiently in one spot. All the women on the banks of the stream stood motionless and were silent as they waited and watched. It even seemed as though the birds had stopped chirping to observe the event. Suddenly, the trout moved a little to the left, and in an instant, there were two more fish of equal size at its side.

Kathleen tensed as she nervously awaited the challenge. She was excited, and she wanted to do this. She wanted to catch a fish and she wanted to try to fit in. The people here had been very good to her, and she thought it could be a way to apologize for her poor behavior.

She wanted to show them that she would work hard and repay them all for their kindness. She wanted so badly for the fish to come to her so she could catch one. "Please come," she whispered quietly to herself, then she gasped as the first one inched forward as if it had heard her plea.

The two brave fish behind him seemed to have gotten tired of the wait, and they swam forward without caution. Just as they got to Kathleen's feet, she scooped her arms down through the cool, clear water and cupped her hands together as they came out. Water flew upon the bank, over the pile of lifeless fish, but alas, no trout came with the splash. She missed. The ladies on the bank laughed playfully, and some of them entered the water to join her. They patted her on the back and seemed to reassure her that it was alright.

Dorothy came up from behind her and smiled as she translated. "They are saying not to worry and that you will learn." Then she turned to walk to the bank. "We have enough for now. Let's go and get them cleaned up now, shall we?"

High on the opposite bank, squatting in the cover of the trees, Thunder Horse hid and watched. He was happy to finally see her beautiful smile, and it pleased him to watch her as she tried to learn the ways of his people. Perhaps he could win her trust and take part in her teachings. He hoped that she would come to love the ways and want to stay. When he brought her here, he hadn't anticipated falling in love with a white girl. But now, as he stood and watched her, he realized that she had cast a spell and he was her victim.

Chapter 14

With each day that passed, Alex continued to grow stronger, and when each day came, Jacob Miller was there at his side. The two men came to be fast friends as they discovered their similarities and like personalities. They found they were both from Kansas, as well, and that Jacob's family had moved to Augusta from Kansas City when he was a small boy.

They rarely ran out of things to talk about, so much of their time together was spent in conversation. As they visited, they also played cards, ate their meals, and took short walks around the ward. By the third day, Alex was able to walk alone, and by the end of that same week, he was told he was ready to go home.

But where is home now? Alex wondered when he got the news. The answer to his question was unclear until Jacob arrived at his regular time, eight o'clock.

"You're coming home with me, Alex," he said with a smile. "I told you that I have a house just south of town. It's small, but there's plenty of room for you." He held out his hand to help him sit up.

"Thank you, my friend." Alex reached out and accepted his offer with a handshake. "I'm indebted to you."

"No, you ain't," Jacob replied. "If it were me in this here bed for six weeks, you'd be doin' the same thing for me," he insisted.

Alex smiled and agreed he was right, then stood to gather up his belongings. He froze for a moment as he looked at the pile of clothes that lay on the chair next to the bed. They were pierced with holes and stained with blood. This was the first time he had really thought about what had happened to him, and suddenly, he thought about Kathleen. Tears began to blur his vision as he slowly sat back down on the bed.

Jacob gently removed the clothes from his sight and handed him the bundle he carried. "*Here* are your clothes," he emphasized. "I'm sorry. I meant to have the nurse throw these out."

Alex looked down at the bundle of neatly folded garments and thanked his friend. Jacob patted him on the shoulder and then left him alone to change. As Alex began to put his clothes on, his mind continued to swim with visions of the painful memories. By the time the nurses came in to bid him farewell, followed by Jacob to take him home, he had made up his mind. "I have to go back!" he announced. He looked up at Jacob as if to wait for an objection, then slapped his hands on his knees to finalize it, and stood. He grabbed his new black hat, then glanced at his friend again, this time with an expression of forlorn, and he began to walk toward the door.

"Well, you don't have to beg!" Jacob teased. "Of course, I'm going with you!" He grabbed his hat off the hook by the door and slammed it on his head, and the two men exited the hospital. As they walked down the street toward Jacob's house, they excitedly began to discuss the plans for their upcoming journey.

As the weeks passed, Kathleen became more and more accustomed to the ways of the people, and she found it very exhilarating. She was beginning to like this life immensely. Dorothy had introduced her to some of the other ladies, and Kathleen learned that the girl she had struggled with was called Summer Rain. The two girls got quickly acquainted, and Summer Rain began to take part in some of Kathleen's lessons. Kathleen and Dorothy taught her English, and Summer Rain helped them to learn more about the Shoshone.

Kathleen learned how to catch fish and snare small animals, how to clean both, and how to prepare the meats to be cooked, dried, and preserved. She was taught where to dig for vegetables and roots, and she learned which plants were safe to eat and which ones could be harmful. When the council met and everyone was informed of when the village would move to the winter camp, Kathleen insisted on being taught all that was expected of a woman of the tribe. She was warned that the work was very hard, but still she stressed the importance of knowing the duties. She decided that if she were to return with them in the spring, she would need to know what to do.

Thunder Horse watched Kathleen intently and admired her interest in learning new skills, her abilities and strength, and of course, her beauty. He wanted to talk to her. He longed to know her. He ached to move back into his lodge and to be with her. "You should go and talk to her," his friend Strong Bull told him one day as they sat on their scout ponies on the perimeter of the camp. "I see how you crave her, brother. She is no longer angry with you."

Thunder Horse looked at his friend and shrugged. "What do you know of it?" he asked in a defensive tone. There was silence for a moment, then he changed the subject. "We will go and scout for buffalo tomorrow." He continued to watch Kathleen as she laughed with the other women. "They should be near now."

Strong Bull decided it was wise to drop the subject of Kathleen because he, himself didn't follow his own advice. His friend knew of his love for a woman, yet he respected his wishes and kept quiet. If he pressed Thunder Horse more, Strong Bull was sure that he would receive a lecture that he wasn't sure he was prepared for. He agreed with Thunder Horse about tomorrow's ride, and the two men grew silent again as they continued to watch over their people.

The next morning, just as the sun rose high enough to begin to warm the day, Kathleen came out of the lodge with a warm buffalo skin robe over her shoulders to shield herself from the chilling air. She found Thunder Horse at the fire pit in front of their lodge as he started to build a fire. Whispers To The Wind was nowhere to be seen. In fact, very few people were up and moving around this early in the morning. The cooler temperatures kept most of them inside their warm homes until a little later in the day.

"Hello," Thunder Horse greeted her with a smile. Timidly, she smiled back as she tucked a stray lock of hair behind her ear. She bent over to pick up the water pouches, to take them to the stream to fill them, but as she picked them up, he came to her and gently took the pouches from her hands. "I wish to talk with you, Kathleen," he said as he put them back down on the ground. He was dressed from head to toe in clothes made from the skins of deer he had killed to feed his family. Kathleen had helped his mother sew the seams to make the shirt that he wore, and she couldn't help but smile when she noticed how well it fit him.

She looked into his eyes with a confused expression. This was the first time he had spoken to her since the day he explained how he had rescued her. "Alright," she said with her head tipped to one side, then lowered herself to sit when he motioned her to do so. "What is it?" she asked when he settled down to sit across from her.

Thunder Horse was lost in her radiance as he looked at her, and he wished he could say what he really wanted to say. He wanted to tell her that he had watched her and that he admired her spirit, her strength, and her courage. She was unlike any woman he had ever known. He wanted to tell her that he was mesmerized by her loveliness and that he longed to stroke the silkiness of her auburn hair and caress the softness of her flesh. He wanted to tell her that he had fallen in love with her and that he wanted her to be his wife. But how could he say these things to her? They had never really even spoken before now, and she didn't know him as he knew her. She didn't look for him when she was outside, and she didn't hide in the shadows to watch him for long periods of time. She didn't know him as the loving and gentle man he really was.

He decided that he would try to spend time with her and show her that he was a good man. He wanted her to know the language as well as the customs of his people. He wanted her to know him, and he wanted to do things for her to make her happy.

"I want to talk with you." He paused briefly, then continued when she didn't reply. "You are well? You are happy with my family?" He searched her eyes, but still received no reply. He hesitated when he saw her expression change from confusion to one of bewilderment. When he saw this, he changed his approach to the conversation. "You learn fast, the ways of our people. You like to talk with the people? I can teach you, if you like." He looked down into the fire and waited for her response.

Kathleen smiled excitedly. "I love to speak with the people!" she replied. "Dorothy and Summer Rain have already taught me some words." She straightened herself up proudly, and a smile grew across Thunder Horse's lips.

"That is good!" he exclaimed. "I am pleased you want to learn. I will leave it to Dorothy and Summer Rain to teach you, if you wish." He picked up a stick and poked a little at the fire as he contemplated his next words. Then he smiled as he looked back up at her and said, "Say some words to me."

Shyly, she cleared her throat and replied in Shoshone, with a standard greeting, "Good morning, Thunder Horse. It is nice to see you today." She felt a little embarrassed and turned away when she saw the expression on his face change to something she couldn't read.

His playful smile turned into a serious but pleased expression. "You know how to say my name," he commented with surprise. His heart nearly skipped a beat, but he knew she couldn't possibly know how much this meant to him.

Embarrassed by his reaction, she quickly got up and went back toward the lodge to retrieve the water bags from where he had dropped them. "I need to go now," she said, and excused herself as she scurried away toward the stream. She fought hard against her desire to look back at him as she kept her eyes forward on the path.

"Why does he look at me like that?" she asked herself aloud as she huffed along. She felt a little irate at the thought of him purposely trying to embarrass her. Suddenly, she stopped in her tracks, and a warm feeling flooded her body as she felt a sense of solace. *He looks at me like Alex did,* she realized. Her hand flew to her mouth to silence the gasp of surprise, and after a moment, she composed herself and let out a chuckle as she dismissed the thought. "No," she mused, "it can't be possible." She continued toward the stream.

Thunder Horse remained seated at the fire and watched her contentedly as she rushed toward the stream. He chuckled to himself as he thought about how sweet her voice sounded as she said his name in the Shoshone tongue.

Just then his mother appeared from the thickets as she returned with her arms filled with firewood. She looked at his pleased expression curiously until he spoke. "She knows how to say my name." He appeared to be in a kind of love trance as he rose and went inside to retrieve his weapons for hunting.

Whispers To The Wind smiled for her son's happiness. She knew that he cared for the girl more than he let anyone know, and his secret was safe with her.

He came back out and kissed his mother's cheek. "I will be back soon with some fresh meat." He smiled proudly as he walked away, in the direction of the stream.

When Kathleen had all the bags filled, she picked them up and turned to make her way back to the village. She looked up to find Thunder Horse on the path ahead of her. He had his bow in one hand and was holding out his other. "Let me help you," he offered as he reached for some of the bags.

Kathleen tried to walk past him. "This is a woman's job," she replied insistently as she tried to refuse his offer. To be near him now made her feel a bit uneasy. Even though he didn't know her thoughts, her face grew warm. *Oh why did that thought of Alex even enter my head?* she asked herself as her chin began to tremble and her eyes burned with tears that threatened to form.

"It's also the job of a man who does not have a wife," he said with a smile. He gazed deeply into her eyes as he gently took the pouches from her. "I will carry my own water." He became mesmerized by her again until she turned and started to walk away.

It was difficult for her to look away from his gaze, but once she did, she continued up the path at a faster pace. "Thank you," she called back over her shoulder as she nervously tried to rush away. Water sloshed from the bags she carried as she clumsily faltered along the uneven trail.

"Kathleen, wait!" he plead, then slowly and patiently walked to her where she had stopped. "Do you fear me?" he asked when he got to her. His voice was gentle, calm, and soothing. "Why do you run from me?"

She stood still and fixed her gaze downward. She shuddered as a warming tingle ran up her spine. Nervously, she fidgeted as she waited for him to speak again. He raised his hand and gently put his finger under her chin to raise her eyes to him.

In his language, he continued, "Please, do not fear me, for I will not harm you." He searched her eyes and her face for signs of comprehension but found only confusion and defeat when her brow narrowed. As more tears formed and fell, he let out a forlorn sigh. In a defeated tone, he begged her, "Tell me what I can do for you." He paused as he searched her eyes. "Tell me, how can I hush the cries of a white dove?"

He watched her for a moment longer as she continued to toss the foreign words around in her mind, then he decided it was time to put her knowledge to the test. A gentle smile lit up his pitiful expression as he found the words and decided to take a risk and state his confession. "I love you, White Dove."

Thunder Horse should not have been surprised when Kathleen dropped the water bags and ran away. He had overstepped his boundaries, and he knew it may take more time now to win her trust and her heart. He did, however, feel a sense of relief. He had told her how he felt about her. The seed was planted. Now he only needed to nurture it and pray that it would grow. He smiled contentedly as he bent over and picked up the now-empty pouches that lay at his feet; with happiness and satisfaction, he carried them back to the stream to refill them.

He continued to smile as other ladies emerged from the path through the tree line and began to fill their own vessels. They looked at him in wonder, and he accepted the stares of bewilderment. He knew that there would be talk among them, but in time, this story of new love would be told, and the ladies would giggle and sigh at the thought of the romance it held. In his heart, he felt that one day Kathleen would surrender to him, she would give herself and her heart to him, and she would love him too. For now, he would take care of her, for she belonged to him in the sense that he was the one who had found her and brought her here. She was his responsibility until she wished to leave. He would make her happy so that she would not want to leave. He would care for her and provide for her forever, and even if she never wanted to marry him, she would always be his. That fact alone was enough to satisfy him for life.

When Kathleen got back to the village, she ran directly to Dorothy's lodge. Dorothy was outside, cooking fish for her own adopted family, when she looked up and noticed the terrified girl as she breathlessly approached.

"What happened, child?" Dorothy asked with concern as she took Kathleen into her arms. Kathleen had drawn the attention of most of the people of the village, so Dorothy took her inside where they could be alone. Once settled, she asked her again, "What has happened, Kathleen?"

Kathleen took in a few deep breaths and tried to relax. When her breathing got nearly back to normal, she let out a heavy sigh, and with sadness in her eyes, she looked up at her friend's distressed expression. "I think," she stated between pants, "Thunder Horse just told me that he loves me." She exhaled fully and held her chest as though to steady her pounding heart.

Dorothy's expression changed from intense worry to happy relief. She let out a roar of laughter as she crawled to where Kathleen sat and took her into a strong embrace. "Child," she said when she caught her breath, "I thought you were being chased by a bear!" Once again, she succumbed to laughter, and when she tried to pull Kathleen to her again, she was surprised by her behavior.

Kathleen pulled away. "No!" she exclaimed as she quickly stood to avoid the hug. "He can't love me, Dorothy! It's not right!" she insisted. "I'm in love with Alex." Kathleen buried her face in her hands and began to sob.

Dorothy rose to her feet and took the devastated girl back into her arms to comfort her. "There, there, dear. I know how you must feel." She pulled away and held Kathleen at arm's length to look into her eyes. "You know, it's been nearly four months since you lost Ales," She said gently, as she brushed a strand of hair from Kathleen's face. "It's time you let him go and move on."

"I know," Kathleen replied. "It's just that when he looked at me and said that, all I could see was Alex in his eyes." She sniffed and lowered herself back down onto the mat.

Dorothy knelt down, then reassured her, "I'm not saying it will be easy, but Thunder Horse is a good, brave, and very handsome man. He has much respect from all the elders, and many women here would love to be his wife." She gently raised Kathleen's chin to look at her. "He has picked you," she continued as she smiled at her lovingly. "He has loved you for a long time, child. His mother and I have both seen it in the way he watches you."

Kathleen sat up straight. "He watches me?" she disputed. "He is never around the village. How can he be watching me?"

"On the contrary," Dorothy replied. Then with a sudden realization, she added, "Ah! So, it *is* him you are looking for! I knew it!" She smiled again, as her curiosity was now satisfied. Then her voice fell gentle and serious again. "Kathleen, I can see the sparkle in your eyes when his name is mentioned. I have seen how you search the village until you find him. I see the relief on your face when he rides into the village after several days of his absence. You can't deny it for too much longer." She raised her finger to hush Kathleen before she could object to anything she had just said. "You can't fool me." The wise woman stood, then reached down to help her to her feet. "Surrender, Kathleen. He is a good man, and I know he will wait for you forever. But why deny yourself of the happiness you could be having now?" She smiled again and walked toward the door.

Kathleen stopped her. "Dorothy?" she asked. She repeated some of the words in the native tongue that Thunder Horse had said to her earlier and asked her what they meant.

Dorothy smiled again. "That is what he has named you. It is what all the people call you. It means 'White Dove.'" With that, she exited the lodge and left her alone with her thoughts.

After just a few moments, though, her thoughts were interrupted when she heard some commotion outside. Curiously, she went out to see what was going on. Thunder Horse, Strong Bull, and about ten other braves were dressed in attire Kathleen had never seen before. Thunder Horse held his mother, and other men held their wives as if they were saying goodbye. When he jumped on his horse, the others followed his lead. His eyes met hers as he thrust his lance toward the sky and gave a yell. All the men returned his summons with whoops and hollers of their own, and all the people of the tribe cheered and sang as the men signaled their ponies into a full gallop and rode out of the village.

When Thunder Horse sped by her, Kathleen's hands went to her chest as her heart pounded with the excitement. The people happily chased after them as they chanted and waved, but Kathleen searched the crowd, and when she found Dorothy, she immediately ran to her to ask where Thunder Horse was going.

"They've gone to search for buffalo." She smiled. She could see the look of worry in Kathy's expression. "Rest easy, White Dove," she said to her in Shoshone. "He will return to you." Then she smiled and walked away to get on with her duties.

White Dove smiled, too, as she ran to catch up to her. She glanced back over her shoulder a time or two, until the men were over the distant hill and out of sight. A feeling of comfort and peace swept over her as she felt again what she had felt only one other time and had feared she would never feel again: love. She could admit it now. She loved Thunder Horse, and she was ready to surrender.

Chapter 15

A cold November wind blew in to accompany Alex and Jacob on the second day of their journey. At about noon, they crested the hill that overlooked the town, but to their dismay, they found it was gone. They glanced at each other in awe, then looked back toward the town. All that was left were the remains of the burned buildings of a town that had met its worst fate. "Look, there!" Alex pointed to the charred stick crosses, which stood in the ground where the churchyard used to be. "Let's go investigate," he said to Jacob, then signaled his horse to go down the hill. Alex was halfway down the hill before Jacob tapped his heels into his mount, and they ran to catch up.

Neither man was quite sure what to expect when they got there, but Alex had hoped to find Augusta still alive with people laughing and talking as they filled the streets to run their errands, do their jobs, and live their lives. He also envisioned a ghost town filled with stray dogs and wild wolves that fed on… He quickly brushed that thought from his head. He had prayed for the first scenario, but was thankful they found it as it was, as opposed to the second.

When they got to the grave sites, he found there were no names on the hundreds of crosses cluttered in the small area. They determined this must be a mass grave, and there must have been one cross for every victim buried. As he thought aloud, he asked, "Who would have buried them all?" He glanced back at his buddy.

Jacob shrugged. "I dunno," he replied as he looked over the terrible sight, "but I'll bet the sheriff in that last town we passed by could tell us the answer to that." He pointed with his thumb over his shoulder behind them.

Alex looked at him. "Yeah, I reckon so." He took off his hat and wiped his brow as he squinted in the afternoon sunlight. "Someone has got to have the answers, and it's clear we ain't gonna get any here."

Jacob nodded, then stated, as if he had read Alex's mind, "I'm happy we found the town like this." He let out a heavy sigh, then added, "I don't think I could have handled it too well, to see my wife lying out here in the dirt, all exposed and such." The two men exchanged knowing glances, and they turned their horses and headed out of town.

After about forty minutes, they entered the neighboring town and went directly to the office of the sheriff. As they entered the solid log structure, they were greeted by an older man who sat at a desk just inside the door. "Afternoon, fellas." He smiled. "What can I do fer ya?"

The two men removed their hats, and as they began to state their business, the deputy's eyes widened with surprise. "Oh lordy!" he exclaimed as he stood and came from behind the desk. He had his hand extended as he continued to talk. "You da one we din't know was gonna make it or not." He shook Alex's hand with a big toothless grin. "How ya doin', boy?" He patted him on the shoulder, then added as he rushed to grab his hat hanging on a hook near the door, "Sheriff Blake's gonna be so happy to see you! Git ya'selves a cup of coffee and I'll just run and git him right now. Just sit tight, now," he said excitedly, as if the two were about to get up and leave, "and I'll be right back!" Quickly, after he put on his hat, he donned his gun belt and was out the door.

By the time the deputy returned with Sheriff Blake, the men had just poured a second cup of coffee. "Hello!" said the sheriff as he entered, and he shook each of their hands. After introductions were made, the four men sat down to talk, and Alex and Jacob got answers to most of the questions they asked. They even got the name and travel route of the kindly peddler who had found them near death. Alex was determined to thank him, should they ever cross paths. After about an hour talking with the sheriff and deputy, the two friends decided to go find a hotel room and get something to eat.

Once outside the door, Alex put his hat on, then paused. An elated smile crossed his lips as a thought entered his mind. "Of course!" he exclaimed, almost startling his companion. He jabbed Jacob's shoulder with his fist, then added excitedly, "Why didn't I think of it earlier?"

"What?" Jacob replied as he playfully rubbed his shoulder as if his friend's punch really hurt.

"We have to go back to Augusta tomorrow!" He paused again until he looked at Jacob's puzzled expression. "I need to go out to the Sheldons' ranch. There is no way that all of the people who work there can be dead. They didn't all go to the festival!" Alex reasoned, then continued in a hopeful tone. "Maybe Kathleen or Joshua, or even Mr. Sheldon is there! Maybe someone from the ranch came along and found them and picked them up before the peddler got there!"

Jacob's expression changed to hopeful relief as well. He knew nothing would please his good friend more than to find Kathleen or, at the very least, one of her family members alive. "That's good thinking, Alex." So the decision was made. Tonight, they would eat a hearty meal, drink some warming whiskey to celebrate, then afterwards, get a good night's sleep in a warm bed. They'd wake up early and head out to the ranch at daybreak.

It seemed to take forever for morning to arrive. Alex tossed and turned most of the night as he contemplated the possibility that the Sheldon family was still alive and thriving on the ranch. He smiled to himself as visions of Kathleen ran through his dreams. She ran to him with open arms and cried tears of joy for his return to her. They would embrace as he kissed her with the deep passion that he kept stored up especially for her. They would smile and laugh as they fell to the ground, and as they held each other tight, they would promise to never let go again.

"Alex?" Jacob's knock on the door woke him. "You up?"

"Yeah!" Alex jumped up from his dream and pulled his trousers on. "I was just getting ready to go get you," he lied. He felt a little embarrassed, and he hoped he hadn't made any noises during that dream.

"I heard laughter. Is someone in there with you?" Jacob asked as he opened the door.

"No!" Alex replied with a sheepish smile. "I just had a nice dream, that's all." He slapped his friend with his hat before he put it on. "Let's go get some coffee and hit the trail, shall we?"

Jacob stepped aside of the door and swung his hand in a gentlemanly gesture. "After you," he smiled, then when Alex was out, he scanned the room as he looked for whomever it was that had made Alex so happy. When he found no one, he chuckled to himself and followed his friend across the hall, down the steps, and out the door to the eating house next door.

It was nearly noon when the two men turned up the tree lined lane of the Sheldons' ranch. The sign at the entrance still had the Sheldon name, and in the distance, they could see people and activity in the barnyard. Alex's heart soared with joy as he looked at his friend. "What are you waiting for?" Jacob asked him. With that, they signaled their steeds and galloped toward the house.

When they got there, Alex stared in awe at how different everything was now. The new house had been built, but it was very different and much smaller than the one that had stood there just a few months before. So much so that the surrounding trees appeared much taller, as did the windmill in the yard. The remains of the old house had been cleared away and five crosses now stood in its stead. Alex's smile faded, for he knew what they meant. As he removed his hat and bowed his head, a familiar voice called to him.

"Alex?" He turned to see a man approach. "Is that really you, boy?" It was Max, and he nearly ran as he came to greet him. "I'll be damned!" he laughed, and whooped with joy. "Get down here, boy! Let me look at you!"

Alex jumped down, and he went to greet the older man. He looked to have aged ten years; his skin seemed wrinkled and his beard was graying, but his hug told Alex that he was still as strong and capable as ever. They embraced and laughed for a few minutes while Jacob slowly dismounted and looked on. "I'm so happy to see that you're alright, Max," Alex said as he drew away. Tears filled his eyes as he looked at the crosses that stood within the house's remains. "I guess the rest of my questions have been answered as well," he said as motioned to them.

Max sadly nodded, then invited the two men in to visit over coffee and some lunch. Alex introduced Jacob, and they all went inside the new house. Max's wife greeted Alex with a tight hug and a warm smile. She poured the men coffee, served them up some plates of food, then left them alone to talk.

During the visit, Max told Alex about the night of the attack. "After about midnight, when I realized that they hadn't come home yet, I sent Tommy to go and get Jake. I told Jake of my concern, and he gathered up some men and went to town to find them. They found…" He hesitated. "Well, I guess you know what they found." Max found it difficult to talk about, but when he paused again to compose himself, he was able to continue. "After a couple of hours, they returned with the bodies, and we buried them there. I'm sorry they didn't get you, Alex. I asked them about you, but the men that work the cattle in the pastures, well…they'd never met you, son. They didn't know who you were or what you looked like." Tears fell as he apologized, but Alex shook his head and assured him it was alright and there were no hard feelings. Then Max gently put his hand over Alex's hand, and their eyes met. His expression grew very serious as Max gazed directly into his, and then, when he knew he had Alex's full attention, he added, "Alex, they didn't find Kathleen either."

Alex jumped up with a start that sent his chair sliding into the wall behind him. "What?" he demanded. His eyes were wide as he looked at Max, then to Jacob and back at Max again. "Where is she, then, Max? Is she alive?" A sudden chill invaded his body as he shuddered and shook with both fear and excitement. He lost control of his senses as he grabbed Max's shirt collar and pulled him close. "Tell me where she is, Max!"

Jacob jumped up quickly and grabbed Alex from behind as he tried to get him to let go. "Alex, calm down!" he plead. "Let Max go! Let him talk, Alex!"

Alex regained control and calmly released Max's shirt. "Oh, Max." Alex's hands went to his face as he slowly turned and went out of the house. The two men were right behind him. Before another word was spoken, Alex apologized. "I am so sorry, Max. I don't know what came over me."

"Don't worry about it, Alex. I know how you must feel, and I know how those words must have shocked you." Max put his hand on his shoulder. "I didn't know how to tell you in any other way, and I expected such a reaction." He paused for a moment. "The truth is, we don't know where she is, Alex. But we suspect she's not dead." He hesitated again, knowing that what he had to say next might be very hard for Alex to hear. "We suspect that them Injuns took her, and maybe other women, too, to make them slaves or something."

Alex looked at Max, nodded, and calmly replied, "Yeah, I hear they do that sometimes." He turned to Jacob, then continued. "I've got to make plans for some travel in the spring." He put his arm around his companion's shoulder. "What do ya say, buddy? Wanna go with me?"

"Yup!" Jacob replied with a look of commitment. His arm went up to Alex's shoulder. He knew the journey his friend spoke of, and he knew it would be a long, hard, and dangerous one. But with his family gone,

Alex was all he had, and he wasn't about to lose him, too. "I'm with ya, all the way!"

"Well, you just go and find her and bring her back home where she belongs," Max chimed in with a forced, shaky smile. "I'll be here, waiting and holding down the old homestead for her."

The scouts had already been gone a few days when the rest of the people began to pack up the village for the big move. It could be several more days until the hunting party's return, and things here couldn't stand still to wait for them. The hunters knew where their families would be, and they would join them there once the buffalo herd was found.

As Summer Rain and Dorothy showed White Dove how to take down the lodge, she saw the angry girl watching from a distance. White Dove's curiosity got the better of her, and she had to ask about her.

"Strong Bull calls her Little Fawn," Summer Rain began to explain. "Not long ago, her mother died. Her father's heart was broken, and he felt lost without his wife. One day, he asked Strong Bull to watch over her, and he left. He did not come back. Now Little Fawn is angry with all of us because we did not ask him where he was going and we did not stop him from leaving."

"Where did he go?" White Dove asked her.

Summer Rain's eyes lowered. "We do not know, but we believe he followed his wife to the great beyond."

White Dove gasped. "Oh my!"

All three ladies looked in her direction and watched as Little Fawn worked alone to take down the lodge that she and her adopted father, Strong Bull, shared. "I want to go and help her," White Dove announced.

"Then go," Summer Rain told her, but then added a warning. "She will not let you, my friend, but you can try."

As White Dove approached with caution, Little Fawn looked at her. "What do you want?" she snapped with a sneer. Her eyes narrowed, and her lips were pressed together tightly as she waited for a response.

"Excuse me, Little Fawn," White Dove replied. "I wish to help you, if you will let me." She smiled despite the girl's anger.

"Why?" she asked as she began to work again. "Can't you see? I am strong, and I can do my work by myself." With that, she picked up a huge bundle of furs and clothes and flung it over her shoulder and onto her back with ease. She turned to White Dove and gave a somewhat sarcastic smile, then her expression became cold again and she demanded in an angry voice, "Go away!" With that, she turned around and walked in the direction of her tethered horse.

White Dove felt sorry for the girl, who appeared to be so young. She looked at her with sympathy and decided that she wasn't going to give up on her. She wanted the girl to trust her, and she wanted to be her friend. She thought quickly, and when she came up with an idea, she went to her. "Please, Little Fawn. I wish to help you," she plead. "Summer Rain and Dorothy were going to teach me how to do these things," she said, referring to the packing, "but they know how to do it, and they are moving too fast for me." She let out a sigh. "They're doing all the work, and I'm not learning anything."

Little Fawn looked at White Dove with a blank expression, then shook her head and walked away.

White Dove looked back at Summer Rain, who motioned her to come back to them. When she returned to her friends, Summer Rain explained. "Little Fawn needs time to heal. We must honor her. This is the way of the people." She put her hand on White Dove's arm and reassured her. "She will come around. You will see."

As Dorothy picked up a lodge pole and began to drag it away, she began to explain. "Little Fawn has already come around from the place she was three years ago." She loaded the pole on top of others already on a travois for movement, then came back to where White Dove stood and watched the girl. "I've come here to trade with my uncle for years and I have known her all her life. She was always a very sweet little girl. But when her father left, she got so angry at all of us." As she went to get another pole, Dorothy added with a chuckle. "We were dodging knives from that girl! You'll do good to stay away from her for now, White Dove."

After a two-day ride, Thunder Horse and his companions found a trail undoubtedly left by a small herd of buffalo. They migrated west at a slow pace, and judging from their dung, they were no more than a half-day's ride away. Strong Bull sent three braves ahead to verify that fact while the rest of the men made camp for the night. Tomorrow they would go back to the winter camp and meet up with their families. They would gather more hunters, ponies and arrows, and the following day, they would all return here for the hunt.

Chapter 16

The wind howled outside as Jacob returned from the shed with his arms filled with firewood. "Whew!" he exclaimed as he leaned on the door to push it shut. "It's a cold one out there tonight!"

Alex bent over the kettle in the fireplace as he served up the stew and cornbread he had prepared for their supper. "Here." He handed the plate to Jacob. "This'll warm ya up."

The men sat at the table and ate in a silence so thick all that disturbed it were the sounds of the fire that crackled in the fireplace and the rasp of metal on metal as they scraped their plates clean with their utensils. Then Alex spoke without looking up. "Reckon it'll be March or April before we can head out, huh?"

Jacob nodded as he slurped up some broth. "Yup," he replied. "I reckon."

Within a few days, the village was moved to the winter camp and the people were settled back into their homes. Upon their arrival, White Dove marveled at the beauty of the hills and rocky cliffs that surrounded them and the seclusion they provided. To her, it seemed as though they had entered into their own private little world. The air was crisp, but the strong winter winds couldn't get to them as easily here. High above, eagles soared, and their cries created music that echoed within the walls of the canyon. The cottonwood trees were so tall, they seemed to touch the sky. Rocks and bushes speckled the ground, providing cover and protection for wild game, making the area abundant with jackrabbits and sage hens. White Dove smiled. She felt at home here, and she was excited to be settled in.

Before the move, White Dove was told that the work would be very hard. It proved to be so, though she didn't let it discourage her. She did as much work as all the other women, and Whispers To The Wind, as her adopted mother, was very proud of her. The day the people arrived, everyone helped each other, which made the work easier. White Dove was more than eager to do her share and required very little direction.

After she pulled the last bundle from one of the burdened horses, she paused for a moment to catch her breath. She gazed in the distance, across the narrow valley, and her eyes caught Little Fawn. She worked alone again. White Dove got Summer Rain's attention and nodded in the direction of the struggling girl. "She will never get her lodge up by herself."

Summer Rain looked. "We will all go to help her when the rest of our homes are done," she explained. "She will not let any *one* of us help, so we will have to all go together." She smiled a devious smile. White Dove loved the plan. Together, they finished the erections of their homes, one by one, including the home of Little Fawn and Strong Bull.

Late in the day, when all the lodges were up and the villagers were settled in, White Dove was inside her tepee. She heard the voice of an excited young boy, who hollered something unfamiliar to her. Outside, she heard the people's excitement as they began to run and call to their loved ones. "White Dove!" Summer Rain called to her from outside her door flap. "Our men have returned!"

Her pulse quickened, and she began to shake. She hurried as she tried to clean herself and change her clothes to go out and greet them. She hadn't seen Thunder Horse in nearly a week, and she was very nervous to see him now. As she thought back to the last day she had seen him, the way that he looked at her, and the way his smile made her feel, she felt a shudder surge throughout her body. Her breath quickened, and so did her heartbeat. She was nervous, but she had to go out there, and she knew it. Not only was it the proper thing to do, but it was what she *wanted* to do. She felt the need to see him, and she felt the need for him to look at her and to *see* her and to *crave* her the way that she craved him.

"Come on, White Dove!" Summer Rain demanded. "Hurry! They are almost here."

The flap opened, and when White Dove emerged, Summer Rain noticed something different in her, and she had to step back to stare. She seemed to stand taller and more erect, like a mature woman and unlike the timid child that had gone in there just a short while ago. She looked confident and secure. She looked like a proud native woman who was in love and was about to go and greet her man. They smiled at each other, then Summer Rain took her by the hand and happily they ran to where the crowd had gathered.

Thunder Horse saw her smile as she drew closer to the circle, and his heart rate increased. He watched as she ran and laughed with Summer Rain, and he noticed something different about her. She looked happy and at peace, and she looked as though she belonged here. He struggled to stay on his horse and suppress the desire to jump down to run to her. He ached to take her into his arms and hold her close to him. He sat tall and proud and watched her until his thoughts were interrupted by his mother when she touched his leg. He looked down at her and smiled lovingly, then slid down to embrace her.

"We found buffalo!" Strong Bull announced, and all the people cheered.

Chief War Dog called a council, and plans were made for the hunt. The warriors would leave the day after tomorrow, after they prepared themselves for the journey and the hunt.

After the meeting, as Thunder Horse and Strong Bull made their way back to Strong Bull's lodge to settle in for the night, they saw someone wrapped in a buffalo skin robe come out of his mother's lodge to get some water. It was White Dove. Thunder Horse looked at his friend. Strong Bull smiled in reassurance, then continued on his way.

After a brief moment, Thunder Horse went to her. Almost all of the fires were out, but the moon was nearly full, so he could see her clearly in the darkness. Her silhouette may have been bulky from the robes, but it was still very appealing to him. He paused as he watched her from a few yards away. She hadn't seen him yet. Just as she reached for the door flap, he called out to her in a voice just above a whisper. "White Dove."

She turned to him and stood still until he motioned her to him. She carefully set down the water vessel and went to him without hesitation. They stood, face to face, silent and motionless. It was easy for them to ignore the puffs of steam that escaped with each breath as they gazed deeply into each other's eyes. This time, White Dove didn't try to run away. This time, she wasn't afraid. This time, she wanted to be here, alone with him.

His eyes were transfixed by hers as he reached out and touched the exposed hand that held her robe. Absorbed in the intoxication of his presence, she released the robe, and it dropped to the ground. She no longer needed it. Lightly, he slid his fingers down each arm to her hands and took them gently into his own. His knees grew weak when his eyes left hers to look at her delicate lips. His own lips became dry when his breath quickened with the thought of kissing hers. He pulled her closer to him.

White Dove looked at his lips and allowed herself to be drawn near. Her hands closed around his and she began to raise herself on her toes to meet him. Slowly, her eyes closed and her lips began to part, when suddenly, they heard the whinny of a horse in the distance. It wasn't loud, but it was enough to bring them out of the dangerous trance they were in.

Thunder Horse opened his eyes, and he dropped his hands to his sides. His eyes left hers as he bent down to pick up her robe. When he wrapped it around her, he looked at her as she innocently continued to tempt him with a look of forlorn. She raised her hands to him and begged him to come back to her, but instead he took another step back. "We must not," he replied with regret. Then he signaled her to go to her lodge, and he watched her as she did. Reluctantly, she entered. Once she was out of sight, he was able to turn and walk in the direction of Strong Bull's tepee to try and go sleep. Although it was comforting to know that White Dove returned his love, he knew that with the way his heart was beating and his blood rushed through his veins, sleep would be impossible. He knew that he would need days away from her before this desire would leave him. The events that just took place would continue to flood his mind until the day came that he could act upon them. She had ignited this fire, and only she could extinguish it.

An idea crossed his mind, and he changed his course. Instead of going into the warmth of the nearby lodge, he turned toward the distant trickle of the stream that flowed nearby. He smiled to himself as he thought of the ice cold water running over his heated body. "I will sleep well tonight."

White Dove didn't see Thunder Horse the next day, and when it came time for the men to leave for the hunt the following morning, he was still nowhere in sight. Dorothy saw her scanning the area. With White Dove still new and unfamiliar to all the ways of the people, she went to her and explained. "Several men went out very early, to make sure the buffalo were still nearby. Thunder Horse was among them." She put a comforting arm around White Dove's shoulders. "Don't worry, my dear. He'll be back in a few days." She smiled, then went on about her duties.

Summer Rain said goodbye to Swift Arrow, and the other women bid farewell to their men as well. White Dove felt sad that she missed the opportunity to see Thunder Horse before he left—so much so that she didn't want to be in the cheerful company of the others. Right now, she just wanted to be alone and go back to sleep. The people had all awoken earlier than normal to see the men off, and the chores wouldn't be started for a while yet. White Dove didn't see any reason why she should stay up now. She knew her mother would wake her when it was time to get up, so she went back inside and crawled into the comfort of her nice warm furs.

Later that day, the first snow of the season began to fall. All the children twirled and danced as they played, and they giggled as they tried to catch snowflakes on their tongues. White Dove lay on the ground and showed them how to make snow angels. She promised that when there was more snow on the ground, she would teach them how to make a snowman. The children continued to laugh and play, and White Dove returned to her chores with Dorothy, Summer Rain, and the other women.

The next day, as the ladies worked, White Dove noticed something different. Little Fawn sat among them as she sewed a new pair of leggings for Strong Bull. The other ladies noticed, too, but didn't make it apparent. They knew that, in her own time, she would accept them as they had her. White Dove smiled as she looked forward to the day that the girl would talk with them as well.

After a day's ride, the second group of men met up with Thunder Horse and Strong Bull's group. They had stopped on a bluff that overlooked the valley where the buffalo peacefully grazed. The view excited them, especially the younger men who were on this journey for the first time. The men mounted their ponies, and Strong Bull gave the signal. Quickly and quietly, they made their way along the edge of the cliff to the cascading hills and down to the valley floor, toward the unsuspecting herd. It wasn't long before the men were detected and several bison began to send out warnings throughout the herd in the forms of grunts and moos. Instantly, they all began to run in fear of the surprise attack, and dust stirred from the ground as the beasts ran in a pattern resembling the currents of a flowing stream. The rising cloud of dirt made it difficult for the men to see the buffalo, but when the herd split, so did the gritty brown cloud. Soon, they were able to focus their vision, and the hunt began. Arrows launched simultaneously. The struck beasts fell to the ground with heavy thuds and left flattened trails of prairie grass where their enormous bodies slid along the ground to their final resting places. The hunt was quick and went well. They killed very few bison, as they didn't really need much meat or many hides for blankets. This hunt was planned not only to secure the meat stores to get them through the winter months, but also to benefit some of the young braves. It was to give them some hunting experience for the much bigger and more important hunt in the upcoming spring. For Thunder Horse, though, it was a nice break away from the torture at home. He was enjoying the work until later in the day, after the bison were packed up for the transport home, when he was approached by his good friend.

As Strong Bull drew near, Thunder Horse could see that he was carrying one of his arrows. As he handed it to him, a smile crossed his lips, and he said, "I don't think anyone else saw you miss that cow." Tauntingly, he held up his hands about a foot apart and continued. "She was *this* close to you!" Thunder Horse smirked as he took the arrow, and Strong Bull added in jest, "You'd better hang on to your White Dove, for if you lose her, you will be no good to our people." Strong Bull shook his head and laughed loudly as he walked away.

Thunder Horse smiled as he slid the arrow back into its quiver. He knew his brother was right. If he lost his White Dove, he wouldn't know how to function. He must see to it that he kept her forever.

After four days, the hunters returned home. Young scouts rode into the village to announce their arrival to the tribe. The excited people gathered outside to greet them. A few men mounted ponies and towed fresh horses out to meet them and relieve their burdened animals of their loads. Within an hour, White Dove saw them as they rode along the cliff that overlooked the valley. She made him out instantly. He seemed to sit taller on his horse than the other men did—at least, that was how she saw him. Instantly, her heart began to pound as it did whenever she saw him.

"Go to him," Summer Rain coaxed her. "Go to welcome your 'brother' home." She smiled at White Dove and gave her a little push to get her going.

They ran together to the edge of the village to join the others, and they got lost in the crowd. White Dove found Whispers To The Wind, and they hugged as they waited for their special man to descend into the village. Summer Rain ran to Swift Arrow, Dorothy ran to Crow Talker, and Little Fawn stood in the distance and watched with a heavy heart. White Dove noticed her and wished there was something she could, do but when Thunder Horse drew near, Whispers To The Wind pulled her to follow her to him, and at that point, nothing else mattered.

The proud warrior pulled his mother close and held her long and tight, then he turned to White Dove. His embrace was short and sweet, and it left her feeling a bit empty and mystified. Then she remembered that everyone saw her as his adopted sister, and he had to treat her as such...for now.

A feast was held in the main lodge that evening to celebrate the men's safe return and the amount of food and clothing they provided, and to give thanks that no men or ponies were injured or lost in this quest. Thunder Horse and Strong Bull announced to everyone the feats of the two youngest warriors who accompanied the party and proudly told how Small Otter and Chases Rabbits both killed their first bison. The crowd cheered, and the boys were asked to share their individual tales.

The stories and laughter went on into the late hours of the night as everyone continued to celebrate. Thunder Horse and White Dove exchanged playful glances and shy smiles.

Several women had gone to their lodges to sleep or to tuck their drowsy children in for the night. It wasn't long before White Dove felt the fatigue of the day, and she too excused herself.

As she got up, Thunder Horse looked at his mother. She nodded to him, and he smiled. He gave White Dove some time, and when he knew she would be in her lodge and settled in for the night, he excused himself and left the celebration. A handful of people knew that it wasn't rest he sought. Each of them smiled to themselves, happy that the proud man had finally found love.

The unsuspecting White Dove lay on her bed of robes and snuggled down deep within the blankets. She had just closed her eyes when he entered the lodge without a request and without an invitation. Why should he wait for one? This was his lodge, and he had every right to be there. She rose to sit as he walked toward her. She tried hard to swallow the lump that formed in her throat, but it remained. Her eyes were locked on his as they twinkled in the firelight. She shuddered as a familiar chill ran through her body, and once again, her heart raced and her breath quickened. She knew they were alone, truly alone, and what happened tonight was for them and only them, to know.

He knelt down to sit in front of her, then reached out and ran his finger down the side of her face to move a strand of hair that crossed her lips. His eyes followed his finger and as he continued to trace her jawline and down the side of her neck to her shoulder, his gaze moved back to her eyes. He slid his hand down the length of her arm until it came to rest at her hand. She accepted his touch, and her fingers closed around his. The thumps of his heart pounded in his chest, and his breath quickened. He fixed his sights on her lips, and as they parted, his desire to taste them grew beyond his control. He cautiously leaned in to kiss her.

Their eyes locked as she returned his kiss. At first, the kisses were tender and light, like the flutter of a butterfly wing. Then he put his hand around the back of her neck and laced his fingers in her hair. A moan escaped her as she leaned into him to grasp at his temptations. Hungrily, her lips and her tongue found his with the loving and intoxicating gesture that she had once learned from a man named Alex.

At first, he didn't respond in the same way, but then she felt him shudder, and he too released a moan induced by the pleasures she created. Soon, his appetite grew as ravenous as hers. He discovered the pleasures she created and was unable to contain his untamed desires. As he released them to her, he discovered her lips tasted as sweet as he had imagined, and her tongue was just as soft. He wrapped his other hand around her waist to pull her closer, and when he felt the warmth of her body, the fires inside himself ignited and burned hotter than he had ever felt before. He needed to cool himself. He pulled away. They panted as they gazed at each other.

Her breath was warm on his face. A trickle of sweat ran down his cheek. White Dove reached up and wiped the sweat away. Her hands went to the string of leather that tied his shirt closed and slowly began to untie it. He continued to look into her eyes as she reached for the bottom of his shirt to pull it up, over his head. He released her long enough to help her remove it.

White Dove felt her heart pound harder than she had ever felt before. She wanted nothing more than to love this man with all her heart and soul and for him to love her in return.

He reached out to untie the laces at the shoulders of her dress, and with one pull of each, it fell from her body to the ground around her. Now, as they sat there together, they both knew there was no turning back. They couldn't stop even if they wanted to.

Slowly, he lowered her to the blankets, and when he laid her down, he gently kissed her lips as he began to untie the strings that held her leggings. Her breath quickened again as he slowly pulled them off. He paused a moment to gaze at her and was mesmerized by her beauty. He used his fingertip to trace the contours of her body. He started at the dip in her throat, then lightly ran it down her chest between her breasts to her navel.

White Dove let out a quiet moan as his fingers made their way back to her throat. She had never felt such pleasure before, and she wanted it to go on forever. She opened her eyes to see him rise to remove his own leggings. She gasped at the sight of him, then shyly turned away.

He knelt back down to her and touched her chin. Gently, he moved her head back to look at him again, and then he whispered to her, "Do not be afraid to look at me." He kissed her lightly. "There is no fear in love." Then he lay down on the blanket and tenderly began to kiss her again. The embers that had become a glow quickly reignited and became the hot burning flames once again. He embraced her firmly yet gently and molded her body to his as the passion of his kisses grew deeper. As his mouth savored the sweetness of her flesh, his hands explored other parts of her body. She was his ecstasy, and he ached to take every inch of her onto him and make them one.

Their hearts pounded in unison and moans escaped them as they gasped at the pleasures that escalated from their desires. White Dove had never known this kind of passion could exist. The feelings he created in her set her mind in a whirl, and she found she was no longer intimidated. Her hands began to move around his body as if they had minds of their own. When she realized her touches would cause Thunder Horse to moan and to kiss her more deeply, she continued. His biceps were solid and so were his shoulders, but when her touch moved to the small of his back, he seemed to melt like butter. Lightly, she moved her fingertips up his back and then lightly scratched him as she moved her hands back down. He raised his waist slightly as she moved her fingers around to his sides and then to the front, to his washboard stomach. A moan of desire escaped her throat. She had never known a man's body, but she knew that his had to be the most perfect example, if ever there was one.

These intense feelings she had were new to her, and although they were intoxicating, they didn't seem to be enough. She needed something more. The arousal and curiosity she felt sent vibrations of electricity to every cell in her body. She wiggled beneath him as his hands moved about her milky flesh, and the moans she emitted became high-pitched as they sent her plea to him.

Thunder Horse paused briefly to look into her eyes. He felt as though he was about to explode from this torture. As he searched the messages that her eyes sent, he found ones of acceptance and desire. She was as hungry for him as he was for her. Slowly, he rose to position himself above her and when he leaned in to kiss her again, she raised her body to him. The union was made, and the pleasures it created sent hot bolts through both their bodies. White Dove tried to cry out, but Thunder Horse muffled her sounds with his devouring kisses. When the initial pain subsuded, she couldn't help but to move with him. Soon, their rhythms blended as though they were one, and the heat they generated was more than either of them had thought possible. As their movements quickened, the flames grew hotter and she began to feel the ecstasy rise as they climbed higher and higher to the peak with each loving thrust.

When they reached the summit, they arrived there together. It came as a tingling rush that enveloped their entire bodies and took them further away from the world and from reality. Their kisses grew more passionate as White Dove began to shudder. She wrapped her arms and legs around him and held him tight as he began to slow his movements.

Tenderly, as they continued to kiss and touch, Thunder Horse slowly lifted himself from her so as not to crush her tiny frame. Reluctantly, her arms tightened their embrace as she held him above her and pleaded in a breathless whisper, "Do not leave me."

"I will never leave you." He smiled and kissed her lovingly. He lay beside her and stroked the contours of her face. Soon, their eyes closed, and together, they drifted off to sleep.

Chapter 17

The next morning, White Dove awoke to find herself alone. Sometime in the wee hours of the morning, Thunder Horse had slipped out so as not to be seen by anyone else in the tribe. He had to protect her innocence. Before she rose to start the day, White Dove relived the magical moments in her mind as she stretched and smiled, then snuggled back into the blankets to try and find the heat that had burned in her the night before.

Days had passed since White Dove and Thunder Horse consummated their love, and the feelings they shared were no longer a secret among the people. A wedding was planned for as soon as they were able to erect a new lodge for the couple, but the winter weather had been unfavorable for the task. The snows came frequently, and most of the people spent much of the day in their homes to keep warm. On nice days, when White Dove's chores were done and Thunder Horse wasn't scouting or hunting, they would meet outside and sit among the others and hold hands as they talked and ate together. They were very happy, and everyone could see it in the way that they looked at each other.

One such day, as she came from the tepee to enjoy the warming sunshine, she smiled as she saw him coming toward her. Something was different, though. At once, she noticed that he approached at a fast pace with his pony in tow, and as he drew near, she saw that his expression was very serious. His appearance was very different. His attire was like nothing she had ever seen before, and his face was painted. One side was painted white, the other side black, and there was a red handprint across his mouth. His long black hair was in two braids, and on the left side hung a feather of an eagle. His pony, too, was painted with black zigzag stripes across his chest and on his rump. As White Dove's anxiety began to soar, her smile faded. As she looked around her, she saw many other warriors dressed and painted in the same fashion. Each had painted their ponies, and each of them carried their weapons. Some held their loved ones as they cried in their embrace.

Terrified, she asked him, "What is it?" He took her hand and led her into the tepee.

Once he had her seated inside, he began to explain. "I will be leaving." He put a finger on her lips to silence her objection, then continued. "There is trouble, and we have been asked to help."

White Dove was quiet as she searched for the words to say. She found none, so she sat silently and stared into the tiny fire as he continued to talk.

He stood to gather some weapons while he continued to explain. "Small Otter will take care of you. When you need meat, he will hunt for you. If trouble comes, he will protect you."

"No!" she cried. She rose from the ground and threw her arms around him. "I want *you* to take care of me." She began to sob as she laid her head against his chest.

She held him as tightly as she could, but he was much stronger. He gently pulled her arms from him and sat her down again so he could calm her and explain. "I must go. I am a warrior. It is my duty. It is the way of our people." He searched her eyes for understanding.

He smiled at her and continued, "Do not cry and do not worry, my White Dove." He kissed her hands, then stood and easily pulled her to her feet. "Now come out and say goodbye to your future husband. You must be brave, too. The people will show you how it is done." He pulled her into a strong yet gentle embrace, then withdrew and went to the door. He opened it for her, and after she reluctantly stepped out, he followed her.

Thunder Horse found his mother outside as she walked towards him with her arms out to reach for him. He went to her and they embraced. She, too, cried. White Dove let her tears flow freely as she looked around and saw everyone as they held each other. Men hugged the women and held the children, and other women held each other.

Thunder Horse came back to her and held her close. "You are my life now. I will come home to you." He drew back and looked into her eyes. She gave him a small nod and forced a slight smile. He smiled back and wiped a tear, then quickly released her and turned to mount his horse. He knew if he stayed any longer, she would put him in a trance that would make it more difficult for him to leave. The other men followed his lead and mounted too. In unison, they all gave their individual yells, and in an instant, their horses were at full gallop as they raced off to war. The people waved behind them for a short while longer, then all turned and walked in toward the main tepee. Chief War Dog would have the answers they all sought.

White Dove remained alone, watching helplessly as the last warrior disappeared from sight. She heard someone approach, but didn't turn to see who it was until she felt a warm robe slide around her. It was her mother. Whispers To The Wind smiled at her, then gently put her arm around her and led her toward the main lodge.

Chief War Dog held a council to inform the people what their loved ones had had no time to explain. There was a family tribe who needed assistance, and they had asked for the help of their Shoshone brothers. As the chief continued to talk, White Dove felt an arm go around her shoulder, but when she looked for Whispers To The Wind, she found

Little Fawn at her side. She smiled with reassurance then whispered to her, "Do not worry, White Dove. He is strong, and he is brave. He will return soon."

"Thank you." White Dove smiled back, then placed her hand over Little Fawn's. Their eyes locked for a moment, and then they turned to give their attention to the words of the father of their people.

Hours later, the warriors arrived at the village of their relatives. A council of their own was held immediately to inform them of what had happened and what type of assistance was asked of them. They were told an enemy tribe had made a camp in the hills nearby. It was a small camp, and the Shoshone warriors were only to make their presence known to try to scare them away. There was to be no bloodshed if it could be helped. Thunder Horse and Strong Bull were chosen to lead the party and to make all the plans. It was decided they would don their full warrior dress and ride close to the enemy camp so they were sure to be seen. This would be the warning of their trespass. Hopefully, it would be enough to coax them to move along peacefully.

Later that day, as they rode toward the camp to send the message, they were surprised to find a group of six enemy braves ride toward them. They each held up a hand, the universal sign for "peace," and Thunder Horse raised his hand to halt his group of warriors. They outnumbered the small band by twenty, so they knew the group was very little threat to them. Strong Bull returned the sign of peace and he, Thunder Horse, and a few others rode ahead to meet them.

Face to face, the men stared for a moment, then Strong Bull, who knew some words of the enemy tribe's language, was the first to speak. It was discovered that the man who led this group once worked as guide for Englishmen and was fluent in English, so they conversed in that language. Thunder Horse was nominated to do most of the talking. "What is your business here on these lands of our family?" he asked first.

The young man appeared brave as he sat rigid and replied, "I am called Elk. My people travel to meet our families in the northwest. We were on our way to your village to ask that we be allowed to rest here through the trials of the winter storms. We have already lost some people on our journey. We need to stop and take shelter. We wish to make our camp there." He pointed in the direction from which they had come. "The hills are high, and there is protection from the winds and cold." He went on to explain, "You have my word that there will be no trouble. We have plenty of food and furs to get us through the cold months." He paused as he searched their faces for a hint of acceptance of his plea, then he continued. "The white man comes to our lands, and we have no place to go. You will see. Soon, he will be on your land, and you will have to move your families, too. When this happens, we will grant you refuge on our lands, as well, if you do this for us now."

The proud men of the Shoshone knew that there could be truth to Elk's words. They agreed that this was a decision for the elders to make, so they instructed Elk to bring the tribe officials of his people to the village of their people. They would arrange to hold a council that very evening. It was agreed, and they all turned and went their separate ways.

Strong Bull and Thunder Horse talked of the situation as they rode back to the camp, and they came up with the conclusion that Elk spoke the truth and that his people could be trusted. Not only was their camp too small to attack another, but they traveled with women and children. To start a war would be a risk to them, as well as to all of their people.

When the warriors returned and told Chief Red Owl all that was discussed, it was agreed that there would be a council. Immediately, the lodge was prepared, and so was a ceremonial feast. Thunder Horse felt relieved that the need to kill may be completely abolished with this meeting. As he and Strong Bull readied themselves for the council, he spoke to his friend. "If it happens that we do fight, will you, my brother, take care of my White Dove as your daughter?"

Strong Bull smiled at him and nodded. "You do not have to ask."

During the meeting, Elk, son of Chief Hunting Wolf, spoke of his family's needs. He told the people that there were more people coming to rest here who would arrive within days. He assured them that they would not hunt during their stay and they would leave at the first sign of spring. "I speak only the truth, and I beg of you, please have mercy on our people."

The good chief heard Elk's words and understood. He agreed with Thunder Horse and Strong Bull that the people were in need and he agreed to let them stay. After the feast was over and Elk's people left the village to report back to Chief Hunting Wolf, Red Owl held a private council just for them.

"The words of the son of Hunting Wolf sound true, and I believe him, but I fear for our people when the rest of their people arrive. They will outnumber us by many, and if they try to make war, take our women and children, our horses and our lands, they will succeed. We need the help of all of our families, of the Shoshone nation and our allies."

It was decided then that warriors would be sent out to ride over the territory and recruit men from all the tribes of all the nations who were able to help. Thunder Horse, Strong Bull, and a few other braves volunteered to take groups of warriors and go talk with the people of the other villages. Not knowing exactly how much time they had, they thought it would be best if they split up into groups in order to cover more area in a short amount of time.

Over the next few days, they rode hard and fast from camp to camp to explain the situation and tell them of the chief's wishes. They gathered the words of over three hundred men that they would be there to support them as soon as they could make their arrangements and get there. Some of the men joined up with them immediately and rode with them along the way.

Upon their arrival back to the main village, they found that more of Hunting Wolf's people arrived daily in groups of thirty or more, and the remaining were to arrive before sunset on the next day. They were relieved that so many of their own men could come to help, for the size of their camp had grown much larger than Chief Red Owl had anticipated. Their lodges extended far in all directions, and some could faintly be seen near the banks of the river beyond the hills.

After several more days and the arrival and settlement of all their people, Chief Hunting Wolf, along with his son Elk and some other braves, asked permission to come into the village of Red Owl. The visit was approved, Chief Red Owl welcomed them, and they ate and smoked while they talked.

For hours, they spoke of their troubles with the advancement of the white man and how the future of all natives was in jeopardy. Hunting Wolf thanked Red Owl for allowing his people to rest there. The talks were long and peaceful, and before they left, they found they conversed as if they had always been lifelong friends. They all felt safe in each other's company, but the recruited men would stay through the winter and until all the people of Red Owl's tribe were gone in the spring.

Messengers were sent back to tell Chief War Dog and the other tribe leaders of the events that took place, and to let the people know that they need not worry. When White Dove, Summer Rain, and Little Fawn heard the news, they embraced each other and shed tears of joy for the promising news of their men's unscathed return. The trio had become close friends and spent a lot of their time together as they did their chores and as they rested.

They often spoke about their men—Summer Rain of Swift Arrow, White Dove of Thunder Horse, and Little Fawn of Strong Bull.

"I am happy with him now" Little Fawn confessed one day. "He has been a good father to me, but I don't want to be his daughter anymore." She sniffed as she wiped a tear away. "I wish to be his wife." She looked up to see her friends smiling at her. "I love him."

"That is good, Little Fawn," Summer Rain told her. "I have seen the way he looks at you, and it is not the way a father should look at his daughter. It is with much love in his eyes, and soon, I believe he will tell you of this love."

Little Fawn shook her head in disbelief, then argued, "I do not know. He does not look at me. I try to make him happy, but many times he looks angry with me. When I cook for him and sew for him, he does not look at me, and I never see him smile. When it is time for us to sleep, I try to do things to get him to notice me, but he just turns over and goes to sleep. How can you say that he loves me?"

"He is your father now, Little Fawn," Summer Rain reasoned. "He cannot look at you in any other way until he tells you of his love. I am sure that he is not angry at you but at your age. You are very young, and he may feel that you are not ready yet to be a wife."

"And" White Dove agreed, "he may be angry at himself for his thoughts, for they are thoughts a father should not have of his daughter. Soon you will see how he loves you. He will not be able to hide it for much longer."

Little Fawn smiled and reached out to hug her friends. "You have made me happy, my sisters. I cannot wait for my man to come home to me, for I plan to make it hard for him to look away. I will show him my love, and he will *have* to show me his."

The three friends talked long into the night, and when they returned to their lodges, White Dove sat and thought about what Little Fawn had said. She smiled when she thought about the love that she had shared with Thunder Horse and imagined that it would be as beautiful for Little Fawn and Strong Bull.

Chapter 18

Thunder Horse, Strong Bull, Elk, and many other braves from all the tribes had put aside all the differences that they had in the past and had inadvertently become friends.

They spent much time together, and before long, they taught each other games, they gambled together, and they found endless topics to talk and laugh about. They shared their differences, as well as the commonalities of their peoples' traditions and beliefs. Soon, the closeness made them realize that a lot of time had been wasted in the battles they had had, when all these years they could have all been allies. "It has been the way of our people long before we were born," Elk said one day, when the subject came up. "Maybe the white man's invasions will teach our peoples to stop killing each other and help us to see that we, and our ways of life, are dying fast enough. We do not need to help him to slay us all from existence." The other men nodded in agreement.

One day, Elk made an announcement to them all. "My father will hold a council tomorrow evening. He will tell us when we will move on to join our family in the northwest. The storms are calming now, and we have stayed past our welcome." He stood to leave, then added, "Your family is welcome to come to our meeting, if you wish."

"We thank you, Elk," Strong Bull replied. "We will be having a council of our own tomorrow. We, too, will be moving soon."

After their friends left, Thunder Horse and Strong Bull prepared themselves for bed. As Thunder Horse lay down, he began to think of White Dove and how much he missed her. He thought about how happy he would be to see her again, when a haunting impression invaded his mind. He tried to sleep, but the vision kept him from it. Finally, he decided to express his concerns to Strong Bull. "Brother?" he asked. "I have a fear." After a brief pause, he continued. "I told my White Dove that if she wished to return to the white man's village after the snows, I would take her." He looked at his friend, who nodded for him to continue. "I fear that she will want to go. The snows and the cold may be too hard for her to bear in our lodges. Or perhaps she longs for her way of life and the company of her own people." He let out a heavy sigh. "I do not think I could take her."

"I will take her, brother, but I am sure she will want to stay with you. Now do not worry and go to sleep."

Thunder Horse lay back down, but he didn't feel any better about his worries. He tossed and turned as he contemplated his thoughts for a while more, and when he could no longer stay quiet, he spoke again. "What will you tell her, if she asks the reason for my not taking her?"

Strong Bull sighed. "I do not know." He thought for a moment. "I can tell her you were injured while hunting and you had to stay here to heal."

He wasn't happy with that story. "If we tell her such a lie, I will not be able to go home with you and I will not be able to see her again before she leaves."

Strong Bull let out another sigh, then rolled over to face his brother. "Why do you not go and tell her yourself? I am sure she has not changed her mind. If I'm wrong, I will injure you myself so that you *cannot* take her." He rolled over again, then added, "Now stop worrying and go to sleep."

Thunder Horse knew that his friend was probably right. He smiled at his words, then lay his head down and found sleep quickly.

That next night, the council had decided that the recruits would stay to watch over the village. When their temporary neighbors began to move, the men would be free to return to their homes whenever they chose. This pleased everyone, especially those with women and children. When such a day came, Thunder Horse and Strong Bull sat atop their mounts, and they watched in the distance as lodge poles became exposed when their covers were removed. They looked at each other and smiled. They stood and observed for a long while, and after a time, Strong Bull broke the silence. "Little Fawn has been on my mind a lot these days. I have never been away from her for this long." He looked down as he spoke, but he knew Thunder Horse's eyes were upon him. Strong Bull continued. "I do not like to be away from her. She is so alone, and I fear for her happiness." He looked up to see a very attentive response from his friend. "I listened to your words the other night as you spoke of your White Dove and how you could not bear for her to leave you. I listened as you told me it would be difficult for you to take her away. It made me think of my Little Fawn." He looked into the distance as he made his last statement. "If she wanted to leave, I could not take her. I could not easily let her go."

They sat silent for a long while and contemplated. Thunder Horse tried to find the words to ease his friend's mind. Then a devious thought came to mind, and he replied in a serious voice, "I could injure you, if you wish."

The men looked at each other and began to laugh, the mood lightened, and Strong Bull was able to relax. He nodded and replied, "Thank you, brother! You are indeed a true friend!"

Within a week's time, many of their lodges already gone, a group of braves rode into the village with Elk to inform Red Owl's people that, in a day or two, the remaining people of their tribe would move on as well. They offered many gifts of jewelry, pottery, and furs as tokens of their thanks and friendships. Red Owl accepted the gifts and sent blessings for the rest of their journey to their family. Thunder Horse, Strong Bull, and six other braves accompanied them halfway back to their camp to bid farewell to their new friends. As they came to the top of the bluff that overlooked the cavernous valley below, the men dismounted and walked toward one another. Thunder Horse placed his hand on Elk's shoulder. Elk returned the gesture and said, "I will miss you, my friend." Thunder Horse nodded. Then Elk turned to Strong Bull. "And also you." The bond that the men shared was a strong one, and they all knew it would serve them and their families well in the years to come.

When the time came that all of the tribes of the Shoshone were free to return to their own villages and their families, Chief Red Owl expressed his thanks by offering many of the gifts given to him by Chief Hunting Wolf. He also gave his word that, should the services of his village ever be needed for anything in the future, they only need ask.

With happy hearts, Thunder Horse, Strong Bull, and their brothers left the camp of Chief Red Owl and headed for home. The journey was long, but by the time the sun was high the next day, they reached the cliff that looked over the valley where their families awaited their return. The men spread out along the ledge and watched as their people went about their daily activities. Thunder Horse sought out White Dove and watched her as she laughed with her friends. At that same moment, he realized that one of the women who laughed with her was Little Fawn. He looked over at Strong Bull, and it was evident that he saw it too. He was awestruck. "I have never even seen her smile," he commented.

It wasn't long before their presence was discovered, and when the people below began to cheer, the other braves began to descend the hill, but Thunder Horse held his ground as he watched in anxious anticipation for the reaction of his beautiful White Dove when she learned of his return. His heartbeat quickened when he saw her look up at him.

She remained motionless, even though Little Fawn tugged at her arm as if to awaken her from a trance. "They are home!" Little Fawn cried, and she pointed as she pulled. "Our brothers have come home!"

Little Fawn gave up on her, ran to where everyone else gathered, and disappeared into the crowd, but White Dove didn't join her. She continued to gaze at Thunder Horse and admire the way he looked as he sat high on his pony. A smile crossed her lips, and tears of joy formed in her eyes as she began to walk toward him.

When he saw her come toward him, all fears of her wanting to go back to her people left him, and the need to hold her became more urgent than he could bear. As the other braves began to descend the worn path that led to the bottom of the bluff, he instead signaled his horse forward. The steed slid, pranced, and sidestepped down the face of the rocky cliff, and when they reached the bottom, he went into a lope toward where White Dove stood. Thunder Horse slid from horseback, then scooped her up into his arms and held her as tightly as he could without crushing her. As they held each other, they shut out everyone and everything else around them. "I have missed you," he said between kisses as he held her close to him. "I love you, my White Dove," he confessed, then pulled back and gently held her face in his hands. As he searched her eyes and wiped her tears away, he continued. "Through this trial, I have found that I do not wish to live without you." He pulled her to him again and held her lovingly. "I want you to stay with me forever, as my wife." He pulled away to look into her eyes. "Today!" he added. "Right now!"

White Dove nodded and sniffed between sobs. "I want to be your wife today, too, Thunder Horse."

As soon as the people were settled, arrangements were made and the ceremony was performed. They were wed before sunset. That night, when he took her into his lodge in sight of all the people, they knew what happened and they approved. Whispers To The Wind would stay in the lodge of Strong Bull and Little Fawn, and tomorrow they would break camp and start their journey back to the summer grounds. There, they would build their own lodge and live together as man and wife forever.

Chapter 19

It had taken the people several days to move and settle back into their lodges. Everyone was happy to be home. The fresh spring air was uplifting, shoots of green grass peeked through the melting snow, and buds formed on the trees. It was a time of new beginnings.

As he and Little Fawn erected their lodge, Strong Bull decided that once they were settled, it would be as good a time as any to confess his love for Little Fawn. When the sun set and they were in for the night, Strong Bull built the fire that would keep them warm while they slept. As the sparks became flames, he sat back and stared into the fire. She waited in the shadows for him to crawl under his blanket and turn away, as he always did, so she could ready herself for bed. Tonight, he was different. She knew something was on his mind, and she feared she had done something to disappoint him. Then he spoke. "Come, Little Fawn." He touched the robe on the floor beside him. "Sit with me. I wish to talk to you."

Little Fawn complied and patiently waited for him to continue.

There was a long silence as he searched for the words he wished to say. Then he looked over at her. His heart melted when he looked into her eyes. He feared that Thunder Horse was wrong and that she did not feel the same for him. He had to know, so he asked her. "Are you happy here…" He paused. "With me?"

Her eyes went to the fire. Many thoughts flooded her mind as she tried to find the reason for such a question. She could think of none, but then the words of Summer Rain and White Dove surfaced, and she replied with as much confidence as she could muster up. "Yes, I am happy," she replied, and her eyes went back to his.

He looked back to the fire as he picked up another stick and poked the burning logs. To speak from his heart was something he was not accustomed to, so it was difficult for him to say what he felt. He tried to change the subject. "I saw you laugh the day we arrived. You looked very happy. I believe you have found good friends in White Dove and Summer Rain." He looked at her again and found a smile on her face. This made him feel a sense of relief, and he had to tell her so. "It pleases me to see you happy." He paused briefly before he added, "You have a beautiful smile." His eyes didn't leave hers this time when he suddenly found the courage to say what he wanted to say.

Little Fawn's smile faded in astonishment. She realized now that he looked at her in a way that she had never seen before. His eyes were gentle; his expression was soft and kind. Instantly, she thought of Summer Rain's words: *He cannot look at you in any other way than as a father.* She then quietly replied, "Yes, I am happy here. White Dove and Summer Rain have become good friends to me. And…" She paused, then looked into his eyes and added, "I am happy here with you, Father."

His eyes closed quickly, and he turned away. After a moment, he decided it was best for him to leave for a while and come back after she was asleep. He hoped he had not overstepped his boundaries with her, as he stood to leave.

Little Fawn stood and slowly walked to him. He watched her as she moved toward him. "Please do not go, Father," she pleaded with tears in her eyes. "I do not wish to make you angry. I only wish to please you." She stopped, and her hands went to cover her face and hide the tears that began to fall. "Please, Father," she cried, "tell me what you want."

Strong Bull went to her and took her into his embrace to hold her and comfort her. "I am sorry, Little Fawn," he said as he stroked her hair. "I tell you that I want you to be happy but, look now." He put a finger under her chin to raise her eyes to him. "I am making you sad again. I am a fool." He smiled at her lovingly. Then, gently, he leaned to her and kissed one of her eyes. As he drew back, he saw that her crying had stopped and she looked at him as a woman looked at a man. He leaned in and kissed her other eye. "Do not cry, my Little Fawn, for I no longer love you as my daughter." He pulled her close to him and held her to his chest. "I love you as a woman. And I love you as a man loves a wife." He pulled away from her to search her eyes. "If you love me only as a father, please tell me now, and you will always be my daughter."

Little Fawn looked into his eyes and confessed, "I no longer wish to be your daughter. I love you as a woman loves a man, Strong Bull."

"Then it is decided," he replied quietly with a smile. "We will tell the people tomorrow, and you will become my wife." He leaned to her, his lips brushed lightly over her trembling ones, and then he kissed her.

Whimpers of glee escaped her throat and her arms went around his waist to hold him. Tears began to fall again, but this time, they were from joy, and they were accompanied by the happy smile that he had longed to see for so long. That night, they slept together in his robes, but he respected her and kept her pure for the wedding night. Strong Bull was happier than he had ever been.

In their own lodge, Thunder Horse and White Dove enjoyed the pleasures of their love in their own way. As they readied themselves for sleep, White Dove went to her husband. "I need something from you, my husband," she told him playfully.

"What is it that a wife of Thunder Horse could possibly *need?*" He smiled at her seductive behavior. He took her into his arms and held her close. She rose up on her tiptoes and kissed him as she slid her arms around him and pulled him close. His breath quickened as she put the tips of her fingernails to his skin and lightly scratched his back as she moved her hands down to the waist of his leggings. He let out a moan and informed her, "I believe I may be in need of something from you, as well. But your needs come first. What can I do for you, my love?"

She pulled away enough to look into his loving eyes, then replied, "I need you to show me what it's like to be the wife of a brave and powerful warrior." She smiled.

"I am not brave nor powerful in your presence, my love, for just the sight of you weakens me to my knees." He knelt down and pulled her down with him. "But I can show you what it's like to be the wife of a powerful lover. Would that please you?" He gazed at her mouth and confessed to her, "I want to taste every inch of your body." He licked his lips, then playfully growled and kissed her with the hunger of a mountain lion.

White Dove fell back on the blankets and laughed as he tickled her and nibbled on her neck. As his playfulness subsided and he became serious, she too calmed and began to caress his back and chest. Her fingers raked through his hair as his teeth worked at the leather strings that tied her dress on. His playful growls became moans of passion as his hands moved up and down her thighs. Their breaths became as one as they panted in anticipation of what was to come next. He discarded her dress to the side, then he stood on his knees and gazed at her naked body with lust. She reached out to untie the thongs that held on his leggings, and as she fumbled with the knots, she grew impatient. "Oh, why do you have to tie these so tightly?"

He smiled as he teased, "Would you like them to fall off as I'm walking around outside?" He laughed as she continued to work at them. "I like this," he mused. She looked up at him breathlessly. "I like to see you want me so badly." He gently moved her hands, expertly pulled one of the thongs, and his pants fell freely to the floor. He was happy to know that the sight of him no longer embarrassed her. She liked to look at him now. To her, he was magnificent. His bronze skin glistened in the firelight as trickles of sweat ran down his chiseled, muscular form. He laid her down on the robes and began to kiss her lightly. He started at her forehead and moved to her cheeks. Lovingly, he paused at her lips and gently sucked on them before he made his way to her neck, down to her chest and beyond.

Her hands went through his long black hair, and as she caressed the back of his head, he did things she never knew could bring so much pleasure. She squirmed with delightful shudders, then breathlessly looked into his eyes as he rose up to her. He kissed her deeply as he took his place above her. She accepted him with her whole body and his mouth muffled her sounds with kisses until he, too, had to release his own sounds of pleasure.

Their breaths slowed, and they continued to caress each other as they thought of the beautiful and passionate love they shared. Once again, as every night since they wed, they fell asleep in each other's arms as they felt the love that each gave the other. White Dove knew that no other way of life could be better.

"Hey!" Alex called to Jacob and their uncivil hired companion. "Look there." He directed their attention to the streams of smoke that rose up in the distance to the west. "That looks like another village."

Frank Wells spat a wad of tobacco through the hole where his two front teeth were missing, then wiped the remainder from his chin with the sleeve of his shirt. He walked to where Alex stood and squinted in the midday sunlight. "That's more 'an likely Crow," he informed them. "We gittin' close to their territory."

The two men looked at each other and shrugged, then Jacob said, "Well, let's go and check it out."

The two men began to walk back to their horses when Frank stopped them. "We cain't jus' walk right into dis here camp. I ain't never been here 'fore, and these here Injuns don't take kindly to white folk. Fact, we gonna be damn lucky if'n they don't find us first." He squatted down in the shade of a nearby tree, then added, "Let's sit here and eat a bite. We best wait 'til near sunset 'fore we go, when they be settlin' in for the night."

Alex and Jacob agreed that he probably knew best, so they sat down, made themselves comfortable, and waited.

Several hours later, the men neared a crest of a hill that overlooked the valley below. They dismounted, secured their horses and then crawled on their bellies to the top to look over. Frank reached into the pocket of his jacket, took out his looking glass, and extended it to scan the village. After a few moments, he spoke in a loud whisper. "I don't see no one who looks white down there." He handed the instrument to Alex. "Here, take a look fer yerself."

Alex didn't see Kathleen either. There were no white people at this camp or any of the other camps they had come across so far. They had traveled nearly two months now, and they were no closer to finding Kathleen or any other possible survivors than they were when they started, except to rule out the few villages that were closest. It was difficult for them to know how far the attackers had traveled to raid the unsuspecting town, but investigations concluded that they had come from the south, so this is where they began their search. "Perhaps we need to go further west," Alex suggested, as he felt discouraged.

The two men agreed, and they crawled back to their horses and mounted. Tonight, they would camp at the place where they had rested earlier, and tomorrow they would head north to find a town, replenish their supplies, and take a break. The thoughts of a nice hot bath, a delicious home-cooked meal, and a clean and soft mattress appealed to them all as they prepared their bedrolls for the night.

"How long ya fixin' to search fer her, mister?" Frank Wells asked once they settled in.

"As long as it takes, I reckon," Alex replied.

Chapter 20

Many months had passed, and the seasons came and went. Strong Bull and Little Fawn were wed soon after they confessed their love for each other. Last winter, tragedy struck the tribe when Summer Rain became ill with a fever and died. White Dove and Little Fawn stayed with their friend and nursed her and comforted her until the day the fever took her away. The women missed her terribly, for the days seemed to be incomplete without the sound of her voice and her laughter. Swift Arrow remarried immediately so his children would have a mother, but the two friends knew that he could never love his new wife as much as he loved his Summer Rain.

It was a mild spring day, and the two women talked as they walked together among the cottonwoods and collected firewood. White Dove had felt pains every so often throughout the morning, but this one caused her to alert her friend. Her hand went to her abdomen, and she let out a high-pitched whimper.

Little Fawn dropped the wood she carried and ran to her side. "Is it time?" she asked, hopeful, yet with concern.

"Yes, I think so. That was a strong one!" she replied when the pain subsided and she was able to stand fully erect again. "Please, help me to my lodge."

As they walked slowly toward the village, they were soon noticed and surrounded by other ladies and some children who wanted to help. "Go and get Thunder Horse," one woman called to a young boy. "They are out hunting," she instructed as she pointed in the direction of the forest. Immediately, the boy mounted the closest pony and rode away at a full gallop.

The women got White Dove settled, and a few hours later, Little Fawn and Whispers To The Wind assisted in the birth of the little boy. Little Fawn brought the baby out of the tepee and gave him to Many Feather, the holy man, so that he could be presented to the tribe.

When Thunder Horse arrived, he ran through the crowd and ducked into the lodge to see his wife. When he sat beside her on the blankets, she noticed his expression of concern as he looked her over carefully. "Are you well, my love?" He smiled as he gazed into her eyes, then moved a strand of sweat-soaked hair from her forehead.

"I am well," she assured him. "Did you see him, Thunder Horse?" she asked. "Did you see our beautiful son?"

"Not yet, my White Dove. I will," he told her in a gentle whisper. "I had to see you first, to make sure you were alright."

She smiled at him as the door flap opened and Little Fawn entered. She carried the newest member of the tribe and handed him to his father. Thunder Horse took him and held him close. He smiled with pride, and he settled down to lay beside his wife.

Together, they held their baby. Little Fawn smiled at the new little family, and she left the lodge quietly so they could be alone.

For the fourth spring, Alex and Jacob set out on their annual expedition, but this year, they decided to go alone. They relieved Frank Wells of his duties as a guide and decided to make it more of an adventure than a search. Alex had accepted the fact that Kathleen was probably dead. The plan was to travel aimlessly, and they would no longer avoid towns and no longer search for villages of the natives. They would just ride until they arrived somewhere. When they came to a new town, they would stop to visit, and if they liked it, they would stay a while. Perhaps they would work for a few weeks, make some extra money, meet new friends, and when they grew restless, they would continue on to the next undetermined destination. Their options were limitless, and their adventures would be many.

This morning, they sat on their mounts and looked down into the valley that Alex had thought he would never see again. They watched Uncle Marcus as he came out of the barn and carried a bucket of fresh milk toward the house. Alex smiled at his friend and said, "See, what'd I tell ya? Just in time for breakfast!"

The two men signaled their horses as Alex gave a call to his uncle. Marcus recognized that voice in an instant, and he dropped the bucket and ran to the house to get his wife. They could hear her scream with joy as they neared, and if it weren't for his companion, Alex felt he could have wailed too. The excitement of being home overwhelmed him.

"Welcome home, son! Welcome!" Marcus greeted the men with a firm handshake and a strong pat on the back. Rose jumped up, grabbed Alex around the neck, and held him tight.

"Aunt Rose." He faked a choking sound as he teased her. "I can't breathe!" When she finally released him, she moved on to Jacob and hugged him just as tight. Jacob loved the welcome and returned her embrace as he laughed.

When she released them, she grabbed them both by their hands and began to lead them toward the house. "Come in! Come in!" She pulled. "Breakfast is ready, and…" Then she swatted her husband's arm. "Marcus, I thought I asked you to go and get some milk." Marcus rushed to pick up the bucket, and obediently, he made his way back to the barn to refill it as Rose towed the boys up the steps of the porch and into the house. While she led them, she poured out question after question, but left no room for a response between each one. "Where have you been?" she asked. "What have you been doing? Why haven't you written in so long? Do you know how much we've been worrying about you?"

After breakfast was eaten and the chores were all done, Alex and Jacob sat on the porch with the older couple and caught them up on everything that had happened for the past four years. Alex told his aunt and uncle of his adventures that had led him to Augusta. Then he told them about Kathleen and the Sheldons, about the time he'd spent with them, then about the massacre, and finally about his stay in the hospital. Jacob helped to fill in the details of the story that Alex couldn't remember due to his coma.

Aunt Rose's expressions went from happiness to despair at the thought of her poor nephew all alone at a time they should have been there for him. They all sat in silence as they contemplated his tale, and it wasn't until then that Alex realized it had been a very long time since he had thought of Kathleen, how they had met and how he had fallen in love with her. His heart began to ache again.

A few weeks passed, and Alex and Jacob decided they had stayed in one place long enough. It was time to say goodbye once again to his beloved family and move on. Adventures awaited, so after a tearful farewell, they were on their way. Alex recalled the first time he had left home, and he felt the same excitement in his heart again. These events seemed all too familiar as they headed out in the same direction as he had so many years ago. The prairie had changed some since then. Alex noticed a new homestead just miles away from Marcus and Rose's, which hadn't been there before.

As they rode along, they saw deer graze in the distance, and pheasants fluttered away to safety as they drew near. Alex inhaled deeply and smiled. "This is the life!" he said.

"Yes." Jacob nodded. "It is nice." They both agreed they could live out their lives like this and just travel aimlessly forever.

Days passed, and they saw fewer towns and farms as they rode along. Then one day, Alex felt another sense of familiarity. Suddenly, he remembered when he had met Thunder Horse. They were near that very location—he was sure of it. He stopped short and began to scan the horizon. When Jacob asked him what he was doing, he replied, "Look!" He pointed toward a figure that suddenly disappeared over the hill in the distance. "We're close to an Indian village." His heart pounded with excitement, and they signaled their horses to continue.

"Should we go and take a look?" Jacob asked. He was a little bit mystified at Alex's calm state.

"We won't make it," Alex told him. "They've already seen us, and soon they will come to us."

Jacob nervously looked around, then his eyes went back to his friend. "Then shouldn't we be running for it?" he asked, his voice a little shaky now.

"Naw," Alex assured him. "Do you remember the Indians I told you about? The ones that I had met once before?" Jacob nodded. "These are the ones. They're peaceful." He thought back to the conversation he had had with Thunder Horse, then added, "One of them is my friend." He paused, then quickly added, "Sorta."

As they moved along, Jacob was still unsure of their safety and continued to look around with anxiety, but Alex kept his eyes forward and remained calm.

*

"Strong Bull needs a new shirt, and we need something for our meal," Thunder Horse said when he came into the lodge to get his weapons. "We will return soon." He kissed his wife and then his son on the head, then turned and left again.

As they mounted their ponies, several young scouts arrived in the village at high speed. When they stopped their ponies beside the two braves, they quickly told them what they had discovered. Thunder Horse looked back to his wife as she emerged from the lodge to satisfy her curiosity about the goings-on. He flashed her a reassuring smile, and he,

Strong Bull, and the scouts were on their way at full speed toward the hill from which they had come.

Once the men topped the hill, they could see the riders in the distance. There were only two of them, and they traveled at a slow pace. Though they didn't seem to be a threat, they could tell they were white men, so they continued to watch. A few of the scouts were sent to search the trail behind the men to determine if they traveled alone or if they led a group of settlers, which could be hours behind.

Jacob noticed them first, and he began to panic. "Look!" He pointed at the group of riders.

"Stay calm, Jacob," Alex told him. "They're just watching us." They continued to ride, and Alex added, "I think we are far enough away that they don't see us as too much of a concern." Then a thought came to him. He stopped his horse, dismounted, and began to gather sticks to make a fire. "I want to talk to them."

"What are you doing, Alex? Are you crazy?" Jacob demanded. "Oh, now you've done it!" He threw up his arms. "Here they come!"

Jacob's anxiety rose, even though Alex reassured him they were friendly and he had nothing to worry about. "Just stay calm. They will not hurt us." He smiled as they drew near and he was able to recognize Thunder Horse and Strong Bull. Then he turned to Jacob and said, "These are the men who greeted me the first time I passed by here, and they"—Alex pointed to the two men on the left—"are the ones who rode with me and led me through the country." His heart pounded with excitement and anticipation as they got about a hundred yards away. "Now I just hope they remember me as well." He let out a nervous chuckle.

"What?" Jacob shouted. He looked around as he nervously rubbed his chin and contemplated their escape, but it was too late for them to mount their horses and try. He had no choice but to trust his friend and stay.

Most of the braves stopped in the distance, but Thunder Horse and Strong Bull continued forward with caution. When they got close enough to see the intruders, Thunder Horse relaxed and called to him, "Alexander Johnson." He smiled. "It has been many seasons, my friend."

Alex walked to him, and they shook hands. Jacob watched in dismay. The two braves dismounted their ponies and joined the men at their tiny fire. "I hope it is alright to stop here. We have come far, and our horses need to rest," Alex fibbed. It was the only excuse he could think of for their intrusion. He introduced Jacob, then continued, "I remembered you from years ago, and I hoped that I would see you again." He touched Thunder Horse's shoulder. "How have you been, my friend?"

The men sat together and visited for a long while. During their talks, Alex retold the story of his journeys since he had first met Thunder Horse. He told of his settlement in Augusta, and he told of Kathleen, the attack, and how he and Jacob had searched for her.

Thunder Horse's smile faded as he heard the story of lost love, but the sad story became his reality when he realized the tale had become all too familiar to him. A small town devastated by enemies, a beautiful girl named Kathleen whose body was never found and the time in which it happened: four years ago. His heart fell as he knew the right thing to do, the honorable thing to do, was not only to tell his friend about his wife, but to tell him who she was. He loved White Dove very much, but his honor was at stake. He could not feel right in his heart or in his mind if he were to hide this man, and the truth, from his wife. This was the man she had cried for, for so many weeks, not so long ago. If she had known he lived, she would have gone back to him then. This man was her first love. Perhaps she only accepted Thunder Horse because she thought Alex was dead. The proud warrior would have to tell them both and then let her decide who she chose to love and the way of life she chose to live.

His heart broke as he translated the story for Strong Bull. His brother felt his pain, but understood that he felt it was the right thing to do.

Thunder Horse swallowed hard as he began to speak. "My friend,"—he paused briefly—"do you remember when you asked me if I had a wife?" Alex nodded. Thunder Horse continued. "I am married now." He forced a smile when he saw the happy expression on Alex's face. He was pleased for him. He continued again, after he swallowed the lump in his throat. "You see, I found a girl, four years ago, who lost her family, her town, and her home." He looked at Alex, whose smile had faded and whose eyes began to well with tears of joy and disbelief.

"You have my Kathleen?" he asked in a choked-up whisper. He looked at Jacob, who too began to feel choked up. "Where is she?" Alex stood. "Can I see her?" he pleaded.

Thunder Horse stood too and tried to calm him. "I will bring her to you, but first, I must tell you." He paused, then looked at Strong Bull and said in their tongue, "Go and get her, brother." Strong Bull immediately mounted his horse and rode in the direction of the village. "She is different," he warned. "You will not recognize her, for she looks like one of my people now. She wears our clothes, and she speaks our tongue." Alex looked to the ground as he continued to speak his words of caution. "She may not remember you. She has not spoken your language for a long time, so she may not remember the words. "And…" He swallowed again. "She has a baby now." Thunder Horse touched Alex's shoulder to be sure he had caught his attention, then added, "*My* baby."

Alex shook his head in disbelief. "She will remember me, I know it," he sniffed. "She loved me one time. You do not forget those that you have loved."

Thunder Horse nodded in agreement. "Yes, you are right." He patted his shoulder, then they stood together and waited for Strong Bull to return.

At the village, White Dove was a little reluctant to go with Strong Bull when he didn't give her a reason why she was to accompany him. She feared something had happened to her husband and was anxious about what she would find. Once he assured her that Thunder Horse was alright, she complied and mounted in front of him, as he had instructed. Little Fawn stared after them in wonder as she tended to the baby.

As they rode back to where they would meet her husband, they met the scouts as they returned. This assured White Dove that everything was alright, so she relaxed. When they came to the top of the next hill, she saw Thunder Horse and two other men she didn't recognize. Her apprehension rose again when the men appeared to be cowboys. It had been a long time since she had seen another white person besides the women and children who resided in the village. "Who are they, Strong Bull?" she asked as her fears got the best of her. "What do they want?" She started to panic again, and tears streamed down her face as she asked him, "Did they come here to take me away?" She grabbed at the reins and tried to stop the horse as she struggled to get down. "Take me back, Strong Bull!" she demanded. "I will not go with them."

Thunder Horse saw her as she fought to free herself, then quickly mounted and rode out to assist Strong Bull and to calm her. "White Dove, look at me," he said, and she stopped struggling and looked at her husband. "These men are not going to take you away. They only want to see you." Her expression turned to confusion when he continued. "My love, they know you."

White Dove looked past him, over his shoulder at the two men. The first one seemed a bit familiar as past memories of her life in Augusta flooded her mind. She remembered him as one of the townspeople, but she didn't know his name. Her eyes moved to the second man, who had dark hair and a shaggy beard. The plea in his eyes had a familiar look and reminded her of a man she once knew. Then, when he smiled at her and sent her a friendly wave, she knew that this was the first man who had stolen her heart many hundreds of days ago, when she was still but a child. She couldn't take her eyes off him as she slid from the pony and slowly began to walk toward him. Thunder Horse held his ground and watched as the two of them met face to face. "How can this be?" she asked him in the Shoshone tongue. "They said all the men were dead."

"White Dove," her husband interrupted her. "He cannot understand you."

The shock of the meeting caused them both to stare speechless and in disbelief. As Alex looked her over from head to toe, he couldn't help but note how beautiful she was and how natural she looked in her new attire. As memories came back to her, she recognized Alex as he had looked the first time she had ever laid eyes on him at the door of her family's mercantile. Tears welled up in her eyes as she reached out to touch his face. Alex shuddered as he closed his eyes and welcomed her touch. She let out a gasp, as if the feel of him suddenly made him real to her. Her tears began to fall freely as she threw her arms around him, buried her face in his chest, and sobbed. Alex's arms went around her, and he closed his eyes as he held her close and remembered how things were before.

Thunder Horse turned away calmly, then motioned to Jacob to mount his horse and ride away with them so Alex and White Dove could be alone for a while. Jacob, no longer apprehensive among them, did as he was asked, and together they rode toward the banks of the nearby river.

When they were able to compose themselves, they sat by the fire and began to talk. Alex told her all that had happened after the massacre and about his visit to the ranch. "I'm sorry, Kathleen, but your father and Joshua didn't make it. Neither did Hattie."

She nodded. "I know. If they had, I'm sure they would be with you right now."

He nodded. "Kathleen, I still love you. I know that you are married now, but I just want you to know that I did everything I could to get to you."

"I know." She nodded again. "I still love you, Alex. You have always had a special place here." She put her hand over her heart as she smiled at him. "Thunder Horse is my husband now. He takes very good care of me, and I love him, too." She touched his face to wipe a tear that glistened on his cheek. "I am happy here."

His throat was dry and tight, making it hard for him to speak, but he tried. "I know, Kathleen. I understand and respect that." His voice broke as he continued. "I'm just so thankful that you are alive and well." He reached out to her. "Can I hold you one more time before I go?" He stood and helped her up, then he took her into his arms for what he knew would be the last time. He sobbed as he stroked her hair and kissed the top of her head. His embrace was strong and tender, just as she remembered it. As they stood in each other's arms, she could feel his body heave as he cried. She cried with him. He pulled away, and when she looked up at him, he gazed into her eyes and confessed, with a forced smile, "Somehow, life was easier when I believed you were dead." He leaned down and kissed her lips long and lovingly as he held her face in his hands. She returned the kiss, but it didn't hold the same passion that he remembered. As he pulled back to look at her again, he forced a smile. Then, with all the self-control he could muster, he released her, walked to his horse, and took hold of his reins, then with a smile, offered his other hand for her to take. She did, and together they walked slowly toward the others who waited for them at the river's bank.

The calmness of Thunder Horse's tone fooled Jacob as they spoke, but Strong Bull knew his brother too well. He knew he was worried about the outcome of this surprise meeting. He saw the relief in his eyes as the couple walked toward them and White Dove released Alex's hand and ran into his open arms. He scooped her up and cradled her in his embrace.

Alex knew he had to come to terms with this reality, so bravely, he extended his hand to Thunder House and congratulated him on their marriage and their new baby. He was satisfied in knowing that Kathleen had a good man for a husband, and he could tell that he loved her very much. He nervously cleared his throat, and with a smile he said, "We became friends years ago, and I hope that we can remain friends."

Thunder Horse nodded. "You, Alexander Johnson, will always be my friend." Strong Bull nodded in agreement.

Alex smiled and replied, "Thank you. I honor that friendship." The four men shook hands, and then Alex turned to Jacob and said, "We should go." Jacob nodded in agreement, they mounted their horses, and after one last glance at the trio, they turned their horses and rode away, toward the distant hill.

White Dove continued to watch them until they were over the crest and out of sight. Then she turned and took the hand of her husband, and they walked slowly together toward the village. Many thoughts ran through her mind, but the one thing she could not imagine was what her life would be like if she had returned with Alex. Thunder Horse, their son, and the people were her life now, and to live any other way would be foreign to her. This was where she belonged.

About the Author

Aly DeRay grew up in a small midwest town in Iowa. She first fell in love with the written word in elementary school, reading as many books as she could get her hands on. Later, in junior high and high school, English and writing became her favorite classes.

After graduation from high school, Aly would find herself imagining stories of romance which led to experimenting with the idea of writing a novel of her own. Many stories came to life, but as real life happened; marriage and children, the stories were put on hold and the dreams of becoming a romance novelist, were tucked away for safe keeping.

In 2016, Aly met the woman who would change her life. Ondi Laure, a friend, began a publishing company and when Ondi discovered Aly's hidden dreams, she stepped up and made it happen.

Today, Aly lives in a small community near the Rocky Mountains in Wyoming, with her beloved dog of 14 years. She is currently finishing her second novel, and preparing herself to finish the other seven that have been lying dormant, awaiting the day that Aly would bring them back to life again. That time is now.